Ring Road 'Safari'

ıyen

Langaa Research & Publishing CIG
Mankon, Bamenda

Publisher

Langaa RPCIG
Langaa Research & Publishing Common Initiative Group
P.O. Box 902 Mankon
Bamenda
North West Region
Cameroon
Langaagrp@gmail.com
www.langaa-rpcig.net

Distributed in and outside N. America by African Books Collective
orders@africanbookscollective.com
www.africanbookcollective.com

ISBN: 9956-726-73-7

DISCLAIMER
All views expressed in this publication are those of the author and do
not necessarily reflect the views of Langaa RPCIG.

Acknowledgements

Before writing this book, I prayed to God fervently to guide me and it was done. I had wanted to use Nigeria, Ghana or Kenya, African countries that are popularly known all over the world. This was because I needed an ideal country to use in this story, where a rich Black American had chosen to dispatch his son to Africa, to enable him understand why Africans keep escaping or moving over to America where they often end up doing menial jobs to survive. But God directed me to use Cameroon instead, the country that I knew best. I followed the advice and used Cameroon, but I suspect that a few guilty Cameroonian bigwigs may assume that certain arrows are directed at them in this book, but no! Rest assured that this is all fiction, meant to entertain and with nobody in mind. I have thus avoided using names as much as possible for fear that some may correspond to the names of certain guilty fellows and cause much unpleasantness. However, if your name is Colin or Tampia, or any name that appears inside, forgive me for the coincidence. If you are Mayor or a high official in any of the towns mentioned in this book, understand that I was simply writing and had no specific person in mind.

The only person I will call here and mean it is Tampia Paulus Agbor, popularly known as Gorille. He is my long lost friend, and if he is not happy that I have mentioned his blasted name, he should challenge me to a bout of vodka. Maybe I should bribe a medic to put him off the alcoholic brew so that I remain one step ahead. The thought that Paul will certainly enjoy this story spurred me on. But Paul, there is no *last fight* in this one.

My greatest friend, Isidore Irvine Diyen is smiling encouragingly from heaven. I am sure I can hear him say, 'Son, you have continued from where I stopped.'

1

Douala

The plane was circling over Douala in preparation to land and I was shocked by the scenery below. Everything looked dreary. The wooden shacks that served as habitation for the creek dwellers looked rotten and desolate. The plane hovered then suddenly tilted, and the squalor stretched to the city, heightened by the abundant rusty roofs. The sprawl of poorly constructed houses arranged in a disorganized manner continued almost to the horizon. From the low flying plane I noticed vehicles lined up as if in an unending convoy. Then the plane suddenly dropped. I felt a strange sensation in my lower abdomen.

My first trip to Africa. I was not coming for work, nor for touristic pleasure. I was coming to learn and see things for myself. One day I had simply asked my father, a very rich black American, about the ongoing massive exodus of Africans to America, when Africa is well endowed with natural resources. In our university, many of the outstandingly intelligent students were Africans.

My father thought for a while. I could see the question was not an easy one, and my father wanted to give the best answer he could think of.

He smiled and finally said, "The first blacks who came from Africa were brought here by force to labour in plantations, do menial work and other work considered not fit for a white man."

"So these first blacks would have preferred to stay in their African jungles unlike now where America attracts them the way flies are attracted to rotten meat?" I asked.

"They did not come across as free men," My father said. "They were actually brought in chains and many of these slaves were even of royal blood. You can imagine the indignity of it all. It is quite obvious that they would certainly have preferred to stay back in their African villages and enjoy their privileged status."

From the little I had read about Africa, I understood that there were very many small villages or hamlets and all had chiefs. It was therefore quite obvious that many could consider themselves as nobles. But then, serfdom was common in many African villages at that time, and it was obvious that the situation of these serfs would not change much as there would simply be a change from an African master to a white master.

"I am sure the unprivileged and serfs did not mind being taken to America," I said.

"There, you are wrong," My father said. "Even those who had no enviable status or were considered as serfs would have preferred the lives they were used to."

"What has then changed?" I asked. "Today, the same Africans are coming freely to America in their numbers, and not roped in by slave drivers."

"A different reason compels them," my father said. "But this time the source is internal. They are escaping to America for a different reason. They are actually escaping from another form of slavery in their own countries, one that is worse than serfdom and certainly more revolting than slavery itself."

"Could you explain that better?" I asked my father.

"I think you should find out for yourself," my father said.

Mr. Collins, who was rich enough and inclined to spend money on certain frivolous pursuits, decided I should go to Africa and see for myself what he meant. He chose

Cameroon because I was a heavy consumer of Kola Coffee which is produced there, somewhere in a place called Bamenda.

"Look here," my father said. "You need to see for yourself why people would abandon a country where they have beautiful women, play beautiful music and good football, and have nice things like Kola Coffee, simply to come here and do menial jobs for us."

"Maybe they are escaping from the jungle, where lions and tigers could stroll into your home in the night, monkeys could come and share your linen from your clothesline, and crocodiles are always there to snap at your ankle if you go for a bath in the river," I replied.

One picks up some of these impressions when watching films like Tarzan or when reading certain books about the African jungle

My father laughed at me derisively and told me I knew nothing about today's Africa. He went ahead to show me pictures of Abidjan, Accra and Dakar.

I was surprised at some of the modern buildings lined up in them and commented, "If they have civilization like this, then they are escaping from mosquitoes and malaria."

My father showed me a close up picture of Hilton Hotel in Yaounde in Cameroon and other hotels in Mombassa in Kenya and Abuja in Nigeria. There were many tourists, certainly not Africans, enjoying their stay and looking far from malaria stricken. This was proof that you could still cope with the malaria.

"Malaria is a problem," he said. "But not big enough to justify the ardent desire in Africans to go away from their countries."

My father insisted that Cameroon would be the best choice. It was Africa in miniature. It had all the comfort, the squalor, the bad politics, the women, a combination of jungle and savannah, the mosquitoes, HIV/AIDS, you name it, and then there was Kola Coffee.

I was thus bundled off to Africa.

The heat almost knocked me down as I came out of the plane. Outside the airport, Tampia awaited me. He held my name, written on a big cardboard, which he held in front of him for all to see. I stepped up to him and introduced myself.

"I am Colin Collins, and I suppose you have come for me?"

"Yeah, sure!" He replied. "I am called Tampia Tambe Agborndiparrey.

"Gosh!" I exclaimed. "Why did you go and get a name like that?"

"My father imposed this label on me when I was born," he replied. "I probably protested, only I can't remember because I was still a baby. Anyway, the old man insisted and had his way, certainly in a bid to appease some diseased parent of his that I never even knew."

"They gave you such a name simply to please a departed relative?" I asked.

"That is a common thing in Cameroon," he replied. "You find youngsters bearing old biblical names, while others are given jaw breaking tribal names because some grandparent or uncle bore them. I tell you, most of these kids end up transforming these names or warning their friends not to pronounce them in public."

"I hope you will remember that when naming your own children," I said and smiled at my host.

"I certainly will," he replied. "Anyway, your father hired me through a private agency to receive and accompany you throughout your safari trip in Cameroon."

"Okay, then," I replied. "I am all yours. You know my name already, Colin Collins."

"But your own name too sounds funny," Tampia said. "Your names are repeated. Only you have spelt one wrongly. How could you call yourself Colin Collins? Here in Cameroon, we only know about Collins."

"Colin is my name," I explained. "While Collins is our family name or surname. My father is Francis Collins. He named me Colin so I am Colin Collins. What is strange in that?"

I noticed some uncertainty on Tampia's face but let it go.

I liked the fellow at once. He was a bit on the plump side, kind of like the Michelin man you find in motor tire adverts, but good looking and jovial. Not one of those dull fellows I could have got saddled with.

I suddenly noticed him gesturing to me with his arm and saying, "Let's go inside the airport."

The airport was architecturally attractive, but signs of leakages were evident. The whole building seemed to be crying out for urgent repairs and renovation.

"I hope you don't need a toilet yet," Tampia was saying, "because the toilets here are not the best due to lots of abandonment."

Some of the smartly moving hostesses I had admired on the plane passed by, probably on their way to a nearby hotel. Colourfully dressed and talkative groups of people who had come to see off or receive a loved one crowded the place, in sharp contrast with the drab nature of the airport building. I started reflecting. If the country was managed as poorly as this airport, then something was really wrong. I noticed there were no sitting facilities inside the airport and realized that whether you are sickly or very old or tired, you are compelled to stay standing if you have anything to do inside or around the airport.

Outside the airport building, we went to the taxi park for a cab.

"You don't have a car?" I asked Tampia.

"I have," he replied smiling. "Hotel Akwa Palace," he told the driver of the taxi and turned back to me.

"My car is quite old and breaks down a lot. When we buy these used cars from Europe because we cannot afford new ones, we struggle to keep them running."

I looked round the parking lots. Flashy expensive cars all over.

"What of those?" I asked.

Tampia frowned. "Most of them are not bought with honest money. Some may have even been stolen."

"Explain," I said.

"If you are a highly placed government official or work in a state cooperation, you can easily have access to such cars, using state funds or money meant for development purposes. Then, there are heavy embezzlers and con men that use such cars as a sign of their ill-gotten status. We honest men on the other hand have to make do with old rickety cars."

From the airport, we moved into Douala town. I had never seen such disorganized crampedupness in my life. There were partially constructed concrete buildings that were already occupied by some form of business, poorly constructed ones urgently needing a fresh coat of paint, and rickety wooden structures that barely remained upright. Once in a while though, you could see beautiful and well-constructed houses, proof that Douala town was actually developing and growing I suppose. From street sides, young boys sold food, items of clothing, and second-hand clothes. The hawkers moved in and out of slowly moving lines of cars, with little sense of trepidation. Everywhere, people sat on crude benches or beer cases in makeshift bars boozing, whereas it was just 11 o'clock in the morning.

"During rush times you can remain on one spot for hours, so you have seen nothing yet," Tampia explained as I complained about the traffic jams.

Vehicles competed with motorcycles, some of which carried four persons. The motorcycle riders did not seem to care that they could be knocked down. They stopped, took off, cut in and meandered without the slightest consideration for any traffic regulations.

Parts of Douala town were well constructed and looked modern. In Bonanjo there was a combination of very old and very modern residential houses, but all were quite elegant. As we drove through the town, a lot of investment in construction works was quite evident. Akwa street was quite developed and a real business centre. There were banks, insurance companies, many big shops and other forms of business activities. However, since our cab was not air conditioned, I was perspiring profusely and wishing I had a chilled beer.

Mercifully for me, the Akwa Palace Hotel had some class. I was tempted to remain in my air conditioned room, afraid of the sweltering heat outside, but Tampia insisted that he was obliged by his contract to show me Douala by day and by night so I could get the real hang of things.

As we sat in the bar of the Akwa palace hotel having a few beers, Tampia explained how we were going to go about my brief "safari". We were going to move from Douala, through Nkongsamba and Bafoussam, to Bamenda the capital of the Northwest Province. We were going to visit the North West Cooperative Association (NWCA) head office where the Kola Coffee transformation was done, and actually visit the small demonstration farm where I would see the coffee plants. I thought that was pretty hectic and told him so.

He took a large swig of Kadji beer. It was interesting to watch him drinking.

Then he licked his lips and said, "From Bamenda, we shall follow what we call the Ring Road. This road leads from Bamenda through Ndop, Kumbo, Nkambe and Wum back to Bamenda. There are important towns and features in between, which we shall visit. The Babungo palace around Ndop has very beautiful pieces of art. In Ndop, we shall visit the Bambalang Lake and you may join the local population in catching fish. Jakiri has breath-taking scenery. After Jakiri you move to Kumbo. From Kumbo, we could take time off to go to Elak. There is Lake Oku which happens to be one of the main tourist attractions in the Northwest Province. It is located deep inside the Kilum forest reserve which is host to the rare bird species known as Banaman's Torracco, as well as some beautiful monkeys. If we have enough time, I could take you to Nwa and Ako so that you move on real bad roads. Eventually we will get to Lake Nyos where an explosion and poisonous gas release exterminated whole villages and all forms of life around it. The resettlement camps of Kimbi, Buabua, Yemge and Kumfutu would be worth visiting. Then you shall have the pleasure of visiting the Menchum falls on our way back from Wum. Bafut, which is close to Bamenda, has a palace worth visiting, and with the permission of the high traditional leader called Fon, we could have the pleasure of visiting some caves."

At this point, Tampia stopped and concentrated on his beer. At last, all the rambling had come to an end. I was fogged. I wondered whether I could remember any of those places he had mentioned. I was happy though he hadn't proposed a standard tourist fare of hobnobbing with pygmies, shaking paws with lions and leopards, swinging on vines with chimpanzees, swimming with crocodiles, feeding elephants and hippos, and admiring long necked giraffes. I had seen all these animals in zoos in America but I must say, it was from quite a safe distance. Many of my ignorant American friends, including myself, I must admit, still had the impression that in Africa you could actually have friendly encounters with these animals as you strolled along village paths.

"Will I see the Savannah?" I asked.

"Sure," he replied. Virtually the whole of the Northwest Province of Cameroon lies within the savannah area."

"What type of animals shall we come across? I hear hyenas and wild cats prowl all over the savannah areas, and cobras and vipers slither around as if they own the place. I am also told that virtually all the trees are infested with mambas." I shuddered at the thought of encountering a mamba. They were reputed for being very aggressive.

Tampia simply smiled and replied, "You will certainly see many types of animals: dogs, cats, horses, donkeys, goats and sheep, chicken and ducks, and others."

"Are you making a fool of me?" I said angrily. "You know very well that I did not mean domestic animals."

"How would I know?" he asked with an air of innocence. "From every indication you seem to think that Cameroon is just jungle and savannah. Well, you are quite wrong."

"You may be right," I replied, marvelling at the magnificent buildings on Akwa Street where Akwa Palace Hotel was located.

"Anyway, talking of domestic animals, are we going to see camels? I would like to ride on one."

"You can ride horses out there, not camels," replied Tampia. "You only find camels in the Sahara and Arabian deserts."

I relapsed into silence for a short while, sipping Kadji beer, and then a thought struck me.

"What of the comfort out there?" I asked.

My father had been a senator for ages. You see, America always boasts of democracy and equal opportunities, but some prominent figures like Kennedy and my father have remained senators for ages, not at all prepared to give others a chance. I had never lacked nor known misery or discomfort in my life. The taxi ride from the airport to the hotel was bad enough. The hotel itself was of class. But I sensed difficulties looming.

"You will be as comfortable as it comes," said Tampia guardedly.

"And what do you mean by that?" I asked disturbed.

"I am simply following instructions, sir. I will do my best to make you comfortable. But your father instructed that we use the common means of transport, eat what Cameroonians eat and sleep where they sleep. Don't worry. Any discomfort will be compensated by the excitement of the trip. Have you ever watched goats fighting or cows being milked? You will see things like that," he said assuringly.

To tell the truth, I had never even seen a cow grazing, not to talk of being milked. I had seen some brochure about Kenya, where half naked Masai were tending cattle.

"Do you have Masai out there?" I asked.

"No," he replied. "We have but Fulani herdsmen in Cameroon."

"I hear Masai pay bride price for their women in cows. Is that what you guys do here too?"

"Here we use cash, palm oil, wine, smoked meat, firewood and even cigarettes. Here in Douala town, the bride price for a wife is measured in terms of imported items such as cigarettes, beer and wine, and local goods of the same nature."

"You chaps must be crazy," I commented. "Why do you have to pay for a wife?"

"It is tradition," Tampia replied. "In many parts of the world, especially here in Africa, some sort of traditional exchanges always take place before a young woman is given out in marriage. That is why we don't have the kind of chaotic situation that prevails in America where divorce and remarriages are quite common and normal."

"You people are simply lucky that your women happen to be too docile, obedient and superstitious," I pointed out. "The American woman is always too fussy about her rights and ends up becoming rather bossy."

"The ordinary Cameroonian rather considers you fellows lucky that you were born American," replied Tampia. "Cameroonians flock to America in their numbers looking for greener pasture. Out there Americans look down on them and very few of them actually make it. On the other hand, Americans come here for expensive leisure as tourists and have all the respect. Those who come in as diplomats earn super salaries and frequent flyer miles and enjoy diplomatic status. Even those who come in their numbers as staff of international organizations equally enjoy special status and earn fabulously, whereas if you looked well you would discover they are performing the same jobs that Cameroonians would have performed better and for far lower salaries."

"Not all Americans think they are lucky to be Americans. It depends on how you look at it. What is the use of being born a poor American whereas you could have been the president's son out here?" I suggested to Tampia. "It actually depends on the situation. A friend once told me that he was such a lucky chap, so much so that the day he gets knocked down by a vehicle, it would have to be an ambulance. That way the same ambulance would rush him straight to the hospital."

"I agree with you," Tampia said. "When I was a kid, our doctrine teacher always pointed out to us how a lucky thief ended up being crucified along with Jesus. That way, he had the opportunity to say something positive for once in his life time and win his way into heaven, an opportunity that many other more repentant thieves never had."

That evening, we defied the heat and went to *Rue de la joie*. This was simply a street where life came on in the night. During the daytime, it looked like any other street and activities went on just like in other parts of the own. In the night however, it transformed like a werewolf, only it did not wait for the midnight moon. Every doorway, which during the day had the appearance of an entrance into an honest home, became an entrance into a drinking spot. All verandas and street corners came alive with activities ranging from roasting of fish and chicken to sales of assorted snacks that go with the booze.

As we settled down in one of the many bars and ordered for drinks, I noticed that *Rue de la joie* was really a place to have fun. If you loved dancing, you could opt for a place where there was dancing. If you preferred just the booze, you could have your choice. You could even have late supper. As you might agree with me, some men can never have fun if they don't have women with them. If you happened to have come alone, there were always women around to accompany you, even back to your bedroom or to one of theirs.

As I watched with a bit of concentration two voluptuous females sitting a few tables away from us, with much of their large breasts exposed, Tampia suddenly said, "If you want to try one of them, just state your choice and I will invite her over." He smiled roguishly.

"No, thanks," I replied. "This is my first night in Cameroon, and I don't want to run into trouble. Besides, my father did not send me out here to sow wild oats."

"I just wanted to help," Tampia replied. "Many young Cameroonians would not sleep in a hotel room without importing a female companion, and you look like a very virile young man to me."

I simply sighed. The sight of beautiful Douala girls was tempting indeed.

2

Departure from Douala

The next day we got up early and prepared for our long trip to Bamenda. I had had a good night's sleep in my air conditioned room and felt very refreshed. I was wondering whether Tampia would not be suffering from a hangover, given the amount of beer he had imbibed the previous evening. Just then he knocked on my door and waited for me to open.

Tampia had advised me to clear my bowels well as the bus drivers hardly stopped to give people a chance to look for a toilet when nature called.

"Any bowel trouble?" he asked jovially. "There are people who develop running stomachs whenever they are about to travel long distances. I hope you are not one."

I frowned at this joke.

"You know that back in America, we travel longer distances," I pointed out.

"True," Tampia admitted. "But out there, whether you travel by air, rail or bus, you always have clean toilets at your disposal."

I dressed in jeans and a light T-shirt to cope with the heat, and we went down for breakfast. After chilled fruit juice and a cup of coffee, I was ready for any trip, be it to Tasmania or to Sakhalin. Tampia had asked for a taxi on hire, to give me enough time to recover from the jet lag, he had explained. It was a small Japanese car, but quite neat.

Moving from Akwa Palace Hotel to the bus station where we would board a bus for Bamenda was a nightmare. When we were crossing the Wouri Bridge, Tampia informed me that it was always under repairs but never seemed to get any better. The railway line in the middle of the lane did not prevent drivers from overtaking on the bridge. The worst thing was the traffic jam that they often caused. Traffic after the bridge was chaotic and motorcycle taxis competed with each other recklessly, weaving in between vehicles and giving the impression that once going, a motorcycle can only stop at its destination. The vehicles were varied, ranging from the latest luxury models to types that should have been put off the road several years back. Although there were conventional urban buses, the people seemed to prefer rickety French and Japanese buses that had certainly been scavenged from a junkyard in Europe. Each had one or two motor boys hanging dangerously from the door and waving frantically for more passengers despite the fact that the buses were filled to the brim. It was equally interesting to note that these moving disasters passed police checkpoints uninterrupted while our taxi, which was carrying just Tampia, the driver and I, was stopped at the three checkpoints we passed, and the documents controlled meticulously by stern looking policemen and gendarmes. Talking about checkpoints, I was really surprised to see the police stationed at the entrance to the jammed Bonaberi Bridge, causing even more chaos in their attempt to get rich on defaulting drivers.

Bonaberi, the twin city across the bridge was quite a sight. I had never seen such backwater in my life. Although the houses along the main streets seemed alright, much of Bonaberi could be likened to the *favelas* in Brazil that I had seen in my textbooks. There were a few attractive buildings though, dotted inside this dreary presentation. The main street was full of potholes and dust and added more grey to everything. The bus stations were no different. Each bus company had poorly dressed agents dragging at people's luggage in a bid to impose choice of bus service on them. One stout old man indignantly punched a roguish young fellow on the jaw and stuck firmly to his traveling bag which the juvenile was trying to grab and take to a bus service, whereas the old bloke had been heading for the one of his choice.

We opted for 'Morning Glory Bus Service' because we noticed that there was a bus that was lined up to go and seemed almost full with passengers. However, as we got our tickets and went aboard, we discovered that we had another two hours to wait. Fake passengers, as we found out, had simply been hired to give the impression the bus was almost full. As real passengers came in, the fake passengers went out, and through this ingenuous method, the bus finally got full and ready to take off. In America such a bus would have taken about forty passengers, but these ones that had been constructed specifically for use in sub Saharan Africa had seats crammed for seventy passengers. The side windows were fashioned to slide open as there was no air conditioning. I also discovered that these side windows enabled passengers to buy whatever they wanted from the numerous hawkers at the bus stations and at each stop on the way, without having to step out of the bus.

The hawkers could have gone into the Guinness book of records because of the weight of the stuff they moved around with all day. Some were carrying goods that could fit into a small shop. You could buy items of clothing, small electrical and electronic equipment, food and drink items, kitchen utensils, toys, pharmaceutical products, educational and many other items as diverse as in a shopping mall. The hawkers though lacking in all formal education, had coined ingenious slogans that could challenge radio and TV adverts developed by pricy marketing firms. Here was clear proof that you did not need to go to university to become a good salesperson. Although I understood neither French nor Pidgin English, I could determine real salesmanship in the language and manner of these untrained – or street trained – hawkers. But I also wondered if they would forever struggle in the street.

I was perspiring profusely in the heat and felt quite bored during the two hours of waiting. I used the time to observe the activities of various passengers who had booked into the same bus. A few seats away, a passenger was quarrelling with a woman who had boarded the bus with three children but paid for only one seat for herself. Her children had spread into neighbouring seats, causing discomfort to the passengers. By one of the windows another woman was stopping all the hawkers who passed by her window and haggling over every item, but never ending up buying anything. A young man across the aisle was eying all the foodstuff the hawkers presented tantalizingly in front of him, with very hungry eyes, and an empty pocket I was sure, for he made no attempt to buy any. Some noisy women in the back were taking their time to buy loin cloth, lingering in their choosing and haggling expertly to make sure they bought at the lowest possible price.

And then, there was this woman with a huge appetite who was just coming from visiting her daughter and son-in-law. She was quite normal, not fat, but with an abnormal appetite. And she seemed to have squeezed quite some money from her son-in-law too. When I first noticed her, she was munching away at a piece of chicken she had brought out of her bag. She was talking loudly to her neighbour so Tampia could eavesdrop and inform me she was saying something about her son in-law she had come to Douala to visit being a rich man. When groundnuts passed, she bought

18

some. Then she called for bread and asked that sardines be put inside. A girl was hawking something in a dish and caught the attention of our eater who bought a large quantity of what I head them mention as *Congo meat*. Tampia told me that these were snails, prepared in a special way. This was not enough as shortly after she bought biscuits. I noticed that she had already bought a litter of some non-alcoholic drink with which she pushed down all the stuff she was mucking up. Our weightwatcher sisters in America would have given a fortune to be like this woman who could consume this much at one go and yet remain that trim.

Finally, the bus kicked off and the driver kind of compensated me for all the discomfort by entertaining us with good music. I learnt it was a *Makossa* tune by Eboa Lottin. Despite the poor quality of the music due to the bad speakers in the bus, I made a mental note to acquire every piece of music by this genius. It became more comfortable as the bus moved on and the breeze tickled our sweating faces. On the other hand the seats were so cramped that I started wondering how I would manage the six-hour journey. I was not anticipating in any way that the sitting arrangement would get worse.

About half a kilometre from the bus station, the bus came to a halt, and the driver and his assistant produced stools from the luggage compartment and proceeded to place them along the narrow corridor or aisle between the bus seats. Then extra passengers who had a special arrangement with the driver came aboard and occupied the stools. This scandalous arrangement seemed to be a constant practice, and apart from a few timid remarks from the regular passengers, there was no real objection. I was alarmed to notice a massive dame settling on the stool that had been placed between my seat and the seat on the other side of the

19

narrow aisle and wondered whether her bulk would fit in. She smiled at me in a very friendly manner and lowered her vast rear into the small space and onto the crude stool. I was totally sandwiched between her and Tampia and mayonnaised with the heat and stench from her body. Apart from the discomfort of sharing my seat with her overlapping buttocks, the voluminous dame seemed to have a crush on me. She kept leaning away from the man on the left and virtually suffocating me. I turned to Tampia who was smiling mischievously. He was certainly aware of the practice of the illegal use of the corridor inside these passenger buses and had cleverly opted to sit by the window.

"Tampia," I said. "Let's get out of this mess and hire a car."

"We don't have money for that," he said.

"What do you mean?" I replied angrily. "My father has tons of the stuff. Let's go and wire him to send money."

"I wonder whether he would," replied Tampia chuckling. "You should have brought enough money with you."

"But my father convinced me to take off with just ten dollars in my pocket and promised to send money anytime I asked for it."

"Your father pulled a fast one on you there," he replied "I have instructions to give you only a thousand francs a day to buy whatever you desire."

"A thousand francs?" I said with relief. "Give me then. That should be enough to travel more comfortably."

"A thousand francs is not that much," Tampia chuckled again. "Its equivalence is just about two dollars."

One thousand francs had sounded like much money, whereas it was just a pittance. "Apart from buying a handful of bananas and groundnuts along the way, there is not much you can buy." Tampia was digging it in.

3

On The Way to Bamenda

I relapsed in shocked silence, compelled to endure the unpleasant pressure from my massive neighbour. Mercifully I snoozed off, but this blissful sleep was short lived. A loud whistle blast pierced through my brain. The driver slowed to a halt and took the bus documents to the policeman who had blasted the whistle. Watching closely I noticed that the policeman simply removed something from the vehicle documents, put it in his pocket, and then handed the documents back to the driver. Thirty minutes later, we stopped at another checkpoint. This time it was the gendarmes. I watched the same scenario take place. The driver went up with his documents and was allowed to take off unmolested, despite the fact that the bus was filled above capacity. Later on, we came across a checkpoint of gendarmes who had packed two luxurious cars by the road.

"This is the motorcycle squad," explained Tampia.

"Where are the motorcycles?" I asked.

"There used to be motorcycles," replied Tampia. "However, they all got broken down, but the squad still remains. Even when new motorcycles are provided, they are mainly used by escort riders."

"So the members of the motorcycle squad have been assigned luxury vehicles in place of motorcycles?"

"Not really," grumbled one bloke who was sitting across from us. "Those are their personal vehicles, all bought from extorted money."

"Extorted money?" I turned to Tampia.

"You see," he said, "when they control vehicles, their intention is not really to make sure that vehicle documents are regular, that the vehicle is roadworthy or that the vehicle is not transporting more than its capacity in terms of cargo or passengers. They simply extort money from each driver that passes by. Where the driver has all his documents and has respected standard road safety requirements, they still create a problem and extract payment. The police and gendarmes do the same thing. If you were vigilant, you would have noticed that our driver gave something to the police and gendarmes we passed, so they'll keep a blind eye. It is just that the motorcycle squad collects twice or thrice as much as the others."

"Why do they have to scrunch others this way? Are they underpaid?"

"They are all gendarme officers, and according to Cameroonian standards, they are among the best paid," said Tampia. "And you need serious connections to get there."

The driver had taken off again and we were cruising ahead, daring the dangerous curves and bends. My flabby neighbour discovered that she had overlooked some snack, disguised in the folds of her loose gown. It was some long smelly thing wrapped with leaves. She took off the leaves in which it was wrapped and devoured the stuff with relish. The bus was moving at breakneck speed, and it was really frightening, especially given the nature of the road.

Then, another gendarme checkpoint.

I tapped Tampia on the arm.

"I am sure you fellows have a very high crime rate for all these uniformed chaps to be deployed all over the place. One would easily believe he is in a military regime but for the fact that despite all these numerous stops, the bus has not been checked even once. Do they even bother about speed limits?"

"We are quite used to all this," Tampia smiled back. "We may come across more than fifteen of these checkpoints before we get to Bamenda. You see, each Division and sub division has gendarmes and police posts, and they all want to make money from drivers."

The next stop was a police checkpoint. To my surprise, a policeman actually climbed into the bus and looked round. One thin hungry looking man who was sitting behind me beckoned at him, and he moved towards us.

"Le voici," he told the policeman, pointing at me.

"Lève-toi et déscend!" the policeman commanded, looking at me sternly.

"I wonder if I understand what you are saying," I replied rather annoyed.

"Let's go down," said Tampia. "It looks like there is trouble."

"What trouble, what have we done wrong?" I enquired, still reluctant to stand up.

"I noticed the bloke behind us making a call. He might have been calling the police post to report something about us. Let's go and see what they want." Tampia was already standing up.

We went down from the bus and followed the shabbily dressed policeman to a corner where his boss was sitting on a stool. There was a bottle of beer poorly disguised by his side.

"Voici le type, mon commissaire," said the policeman, executing a clumsy military salute.

"Donne-moi ta carte d'identité," he said to me rudely.

I turned to Tampia for help.

"Il ne comprend pas français," Tampia told the superintendent of police.

The police chief was wearing a very faded sky blue jacket with a dirty brownish T-shirt inside that could have once been white. To my surprise he turned to English. It was heavily accented but clear enough to be understood. Tampia later on told me that the police chief had certainly worked in the Anglophone part of Cameroon for long.

"Are you the blighter who has been asking terrible questions about the Cameroonian police and gendarmes?" he snapped.

"I don't understand," I replied simply.

"You will understand when I would have finished with you. You were probing into how we operate. Are you a spy?" he asked.

"We were simply discussing," Tampia proceeded to explain.

"Who asked you to talk?" the policeman barked at Tampia. "I will have to book you in too as an accomplice. Let me have your identity cards."

Tampia removed a small laminated identification document from his pocket and handed it to the policeman. I was quick to notice that Tampia had disguised a crispy greenish banknote in the hand that was handing over the card.

"My friend forgot his wallet in the bar where we had a drink at the bus stop," Tampia explained as he handed over the disguised bribe. "Anyway, we shall still see you on our way back tomorrow."

The policeman slipped the money furtively into his pocket and while still frowning handed back the identification document to Tampia without bothering to look at it.

"I will let you go this once," he said loudly. "But no more questions about the Cameroonian police. Choose some other topic of discussion during your trip and leave out honest and hardworking policemen."

As we went back to our seats, I noticed the disappointed look on the face of the informant sitting behind me.

The bus lurched forward as the driver seemed to be bent on gaining lost time. There was total silence in the bus, as if each passenger were ruminating over the incident that had taken place involving Tampia and me, wondering about what crime I might have committed. Tampia cautioned me to remain silent until we got to Melong where the bus stops for about thirty minutes so passengers can have a bite.

At Melong, Tampia introduced me to *soya*, grilled meat with hot pepper sauce. There was roasted plantain, yams and sweet potatoes to choose from. My massive neighbour in the bus made a beeline for roast fish and some of those snacks wrapped in leaves she had been munching at in the bus. I later learnt it is made of cassava and called *bobollo*.

When we sat down with our *soya* and Kadji beer, I asked Tampia to explain what had transpired in front of the police chief.

He was munching on some tough piece of *soya*.

"Our arrival had been heralded by that old wizard who is seated behind you. I had overheard him kind of reporting us to some authority or something like that, but was not too sure. The policemen were thus waiting for a dangerous spy who was trying to document how the police operate in Cameroon."

I laughed at this and asked, "Then how did that sordid police chief let us off so lightly?"

"That is where I had to act smart," said Tampia. "Instead of the usual one thousand francs, I gave a shiny five thousand francs note. I even avoided letting him know that you are an American, otherwise he would have insisted on a lot more money. Anyway, with that money in his pocket, that policeman was capable of developing any plausible story to justify to hierarchy why he had let go the suspected spy. If on the other hand things had dragged right to the police office in town, it would have become quite complicated, and you might have ended up being detained under very squalid conditions until your embassy intervened."

The journey from Melong to Bamenda was rather uneventful apart from the numerous police and gendarme checkpoints. I noticed however that the shifty eyed informant had not come back on board. Good riddance.

After the vehicle had roared on for several hours, it started facing difficult terrain. The steep gradient considerably reduced the speed of the bus. When we finally crossed a small stream that depicted the boundary between the West and Northwest Provinces, the bus whined up the hill to Santa town. The excess human cargo, added to the excessive cargo expertly packed in the luggage compartment of the bus, was weighing heavily on its engine, and in Santa town vapour from the engine indicated there was overheat. The driver stopped the vehicle and jumped down. He and his assistant went looking for water. After thirty minutes of searching, they came back with their receptacles empty, complaining there was no water. From where I was standing, I could easily see two public taps.

"What do these guys mean by no water?" I asked Tampia. "This place certainly has pipe born water. Look at the public taps over there, an indication that there should be water flowing."

"The stand taps don't mean anything," said Tampia. Most of the time, no water flows out of them."

"Aah, the taps are bad then." I thought I had understood. "Why don't they repair them?"

"The taps are in very good working condition," Tampia said. "The problem is the water. The level is often so low that very little actually flows to the population."

"Then there should be a serious problem at the source," I said. I had done a bit of engineering studies and understood such things.

"The sources are located within a forest of eucalyptus trees, and the forest constitutes a government reserve. Studies have proven that the water shortage is mainly due to the proliferation of eucalyptus trees around the water sources."

"Is that a fact?" I asked. "Is it proven that eucalyptus trees are not good around water sources?" I knew very little about eucalyptus trees.

"In Cameroon, every little child knows that," Tampia replied. "The eucalyptus tree sends its roots very far and consumes all the water it can reach. That is why it is used like a magic to dry up swampland."

"That is easy then," I said. "They simply need to eliminate the eucalyptus trees and plant water friendly trees to provide natural cover."

"And that is just what the people of Santa have been trying to do," said Tampia. "Santa town and neighbouring villages that depend on this water have a population close to twenty-five thousand persons, so they are eager to see their water problem solved. They even developed a huge nursery of water friendly trees."

"What is holding them back then?" I was not sure I could understand why a simple thing like eliminating eucalyptus trees to solve an important problem like water shortage would be complicated.

"They need to eliminate all the eucalyptus trees around water sources before planting water friendly trees, but they cannot touch any tree in that reserve without the Minister's permission. Even the representative of the Minister in this Province has no say in the matter," Tampia explained

"But that is simple," I said. "They should simply go to the Minister and get it. I am sure no Minister would want to see so many persons suffering from such serious water shortages without providing a fast solution."

"That is what you think," replied Tampia. "But nothing concerning a minister here is that simple. The minister is out there far away in Yaounde, surrounded by a wonderful bureaucratic system that delays every file that has to pass through there. The simple thing would have been to authorize the Provincial representative to handle it. Those chaps out there around the Minister simply want to show how important they are and are not much bothered whether the people of Santa are dying of waterborne diseases or some other ailments resulting from poor hygiene."

The driver of the bus had finally fetched some dirty water from a ditch and risked using it to cool the engine of the vehicle, so we could move on to Bamenda.

4

Bamenda at Last

Bamenda at last! This was the capital of the North West Province of Cameroon and the source of Kola Coffee. We hired a taxi from the bus station and stopped somewhere at a busy street which Tampia told me was called 'Commercial Avenue'. This street is wide enough, with several lanes on both sides, but drivers had opted to use only one on each side and use the other lanes as parking space, despite the fact that there were often traffic jams. I was further informed that all installations of high officials and some cultural and social manifestations were held at an elaborate grandstand along this street, and this was often. Thus, circulation on this most important and most strategic street in Bamenda was often disturbed for hours. There were quite a number of solid buildings on both sides of the street, with all the empty space taken up by containers that had been transformed into shops.

I was thinking of going to the best hotel in town to lodge and have a deserved rest. I knew from the tourist guide on Cameroon that I had been reading on the plane that there were a few good hotels that could meet certain standards.

Tampia had other plans. We were to stay at his uncle's so that I could have a taste of how well to do people lived in Bamenda. His uncle had been a minister for a considerable period and had thus amassed some wealth to thrive on. Now, he had imposed himself as a Member of Parliament, thus depriving other party hopefuls from the opportunity of equally handling a juicy position. He was considered by the local population as rich and well placed. I had understood that I was totally in the hands of Tampia, so I went along. Tampia's uncle was very pleased to see us and asked us to feel at home. He waved aside supper and decided to take us out for a treat.

The gentleman took us to a joint where we could have beer without loud music. In Bamenda, it is believed that loud music attracts customers, thus making it difficult to find a joint where loud music is not the order of the day. This particular place was called 'Bamboo house' and Tampia's uncle chose it because they had good whiskey and wines although they are more expensive. There was as much grilled chicken and fish as we could eat, and beer was flowing. Tampia was mucking down the stuff as if he were Bachus himself. The most interesting aspect was the conversation.

"So you are a representative of the people," I asked Tampia's uncle.

"Yes. I was democratically elected," he insisted.

I did not see any reason for the insistence, so I continued innocently.

"I hear elections are often rigged in African countries by the political parties in power."

"Rig is a very strong word," replied the honourable gentleman. "We simply correct results from the polls to save ignorant electorates from the dark prospect of erroneously electing inexperienced Parliamentarians from parties of the opposition."

"Why do you do that?" I asked.

"As Parliamentarians of the ruling party, we at times succeed in fitting roads, schools, health centres and other good things into the national budget. The government would not provide such things to an area controlled by Parliamentarians of the opposition."

That was interesting.

"What do you do in parliament?" I asked

"Not much really. We clap and we vote." He smiled.

"I suppose there is not much haggling like in the Knesset or some of those European parliaments."

"What for?" he replied. "The party has always sent in laws that have been well worked on. All we need to do is simply vote and adopt."

"Your party sends in all the bills to parliament?" I asked.

"The president of the country is equally the president of the party. Whatever bill he sends to parliament is considered by us as from the party. We are therefore obliged to vote for it."

"Obliged?"

"Obliged by the fact that the bills are always good and perfect."

"Are you saying that everything that is tabled by the executive is perfect?

"Sure. For example, the other time we received a very good bill limiting tenure of office by a president to two terms as it is in some democratic countries. Of course, we all clapped and adopted it. After a while we received an even better bill, lifting off the two terms restriction so that any experienced and good president could continue in office if the people so wished. The heavy applause that came from the floor showed how eager we were to approve it. We again clapped and adopted it."

I immediately spotted a serious contradiction in his point but refrained from digging right in, rather limiting myself to a simple question.

"But why would you want to keep one man at the helm forever?"

"We don't want adventurers coming in. Our man has proven his worth, so he should stay there. You see, our man is stainless. If you see any wrongdoing, it is certainly behind his back. There are high government officials, and even some tribesmen and close relatives that are overly inconsiderate and greedy, overzealous or overprotective. These often end up committing grave errors that are often falsely attributed to the president. We all revere him but in most cases distrust most of the high party hierarchy around him, whom we consider as mere fortune hunters."

"But are you not one of the high party officials?" I could not help asking.

"No," he said emphatically "I am a representative of the people."

"So he is one of the best presidents in Africa?" I asked.

"The best, I tell you. We have peace, development and many of our children are in universities. There is a lot of money circulating, it is just that you need to be smart enough like us, to grab as much as you want."

"Then why are many Cameroonians escaping to Europe and America?"

"You were saying?" he asked looking at me sternly.

"I was saying that democracy is seriously trampled upon in the third world." I thought it was evident.

"What do you know about democracy?" Tampia's uncle asked. "Out there in America all you do is criticize, yet a few families control you. Obama may have made a breakthrough from nowhere, but the general tendency is that a few big families like the Kennedys, the Bushes and Clintons virtually have monopoly over this most coveted post of president. Even in congress and the senate, there are a few big families that have control."

"No! That is not true," I said. "Anybody can become congressman, senator or president of America."

"Not anybody," said the honourable gentleman with emphases. "A poor man has no chance and coloured men, even the very rich ones have very limited chances."

"But the procedure for electing a president is fair," I pointed out. "We don't have one person being the player and referee at the same time."

"What is the difference with what we have here?" asked Tampia's uncle. "We have an independent body that has been created to organize elections. Isn't that democratic enough?"

"Don't listen to what my uncle is saying," said Tampia. "What we have here in Cameroon is not as independent as an electoral commission should be. In fact, it is not independent at all. It is managed by members of the ruling party and still has government appointees to declare election results."

"Don't put your mouth into something you know very little about," Tampia's uncle said sternly to him. "We are the lawmakers and we know what is good for Cameroon. Democracy must be controlled otherwise it will go out of hand."

"These laws simply pass because you have absolute majority in the House of Assembly," Tampia insisted. "These laws are not democratically passed."

"We have absolute majority because we were elected by the people. I tell you, this is a legitimate House of Assembly and our decisions are valid."

"Uncle," said Tampia. "I don't mean to hurt you, but you will agree with me that your party cannot win elections fairly in this Province."

"What of the whole of Cameroon?" Tampia's uncle asked.

I thought I should step in before things went out of hand.

"Sir, let's agree first that there is a lot to learn about democracy here in Cameroon, just like in most other African countries."

"Young man," said Tampia's uncle, "let me point out something to prove that you guys know nothing about democracy."

"I am listening, sir." I said.

"Have you followed what is going on in FIFA?

Not being an ardent football fan, I knew little about happenings in FIFA and wondered what FIFA had to do with democracy.

"FIFA," Tampia's uncle continued, "is the top organizing and management body of international football. All the big democracies are members of this football federation, yet when it comes to election at the top, democracy is seriously flaunted. Could you imagine that for the most recent election of the FIFA president, there was a unique candidate imposed upon everybody? And that is not all. He is quite an old man and is going in for his fourth term in office. There, that is democracy for you."

"Is there anything wrong with that?"

"Everything is wrong," said Tampia's uncle. Is management of this football federation so complex that he is the only person capable of managing it? The other time, a Cameroonian attempted to compete for this position and an undemocratic process blocked him from succeeding. Why do you people raise eyebrows only in our president's case?"

"If everything is fine out here as you insist, then why do so many Cameroonians escape to other countries?" I repeated the question I had earlier suppressed.

"They are not escaping. It is simply a development strategy. The children of poor people go there, work and send money back here to help their desperate folk. That way, lots

34

of money comes into the country and the poor can cope. Most of us who are rich simply send our children out to study. We pay for their fees and provide them with ample sustenance allowances. They neither need to work nor send us money. After studies, they come back and we fit them into high positions of power."

Tampia's uncle took a sip from his glass and held it out for Tampia to refill.

"This is good whisky," he said with satisfaction. It was Jack Daniels.

I was getting used to taking things as they came, so that night, I fully relaxed in the room we were given and slept soundly till the next day, despite the fact that I had to share the bed with Tampia. I slept so soundly that I did not realize until I woke that Tampia snores like the spluttering engine of an old lorry.

Breakfast was a big affair. There was scrambled eggs enriched with canned sardine from Morocco, fresh locally made cheese and imported butter, not margarine that most Cameroonians use for smearing on their bread. To my disappointment however, among the array of beverages, ranging from Lipton tea, lemon tea, and Nescafe to imported cocoa beverages, I found no Kola coffee. As the others made tea for themselves, I took water. Our host's wife expressed surprise, so I explained that I could not drink anything else in the land of Kola coffee.

"Kola coffee?" she scoffed. "But that is made just here in Bamenda. I don't serve cheap local coffee and tea to my guests. I go for quality imported stuff. Just look at my table and you can have your pick."

Our host wanted to know what was so wonderful about Kola coffee.

"Cameroon coffee is wonderful but Kola coffee is special," I replied. "It is made from organic Arabica coffee beans. The coffee is grown in the rich volcanic soils of the Northwest Province of Cameroon, alongside Kolanut trees. It is quite natural, and if well refined meets very high standards."

I was reciting from some literature I had read on the attractive packaging and memorized.

"Because of the rich flavour and taste," I continued, no longer reciting from an advert this time, "a man in America or Europe would be prepared to offer anything just to have a cup of it. It is because of products like Kola coffee that coffee is ranked as the world's second most popular drink after water. To find an enlightened woman like madam condemning it is embarrassing as it gives the impression that good things can never come from Africa."

"It is a pity we always abandon nice African things and go for imported alternatives," said the Parliamentarian in a hushed undertone so his voice would not carry to his wife. "Tampia, you can imagine that it is a perfect stranger telling us about the qualities of our coffee."

5

A Stranger in Bamenda

Tampia had decided we would spend the day in Bamenda town so I could visit many places. To my disappointment, he turned down an offer from his uncle to put one of his vehicles at our disposal.

Tampia's uncle lived about a hundred meters from tarred road and it had rained heavily in the night. We were thus obliged to plough through thick mud, and if I were not very athletic, I would have landed on my buttocks a few times. My shoes were quite a sight by the time we got to the tarred road, although Tampia had managed it through without much mud on his. Practice makes perfect, I concluded.

"Global warming is turning things upside down. The rains now are so heavy we've no choice but to cope with this impressive mud." Tampia said.

After hailing taxis for thirty minutes, Tampia observed that we should have stayed on in the house until after rush hour. Between 7am and 9am, people rush to work and children to school. It is thus quite a headache to get unoccupied taxi space. The words 'unoccupied taxi space' may need to be explained here. Unlike in America, where you hail a taxi just for yourself, and it uses a meter to determine your fare, in Bamenda, stopping a taxi means you are going for a seat and this has a standard rate. You could propose something less if your journey is short or something more if the journey is too long and you need to convince the driver to take you along. As we stood waiting for a cab with space for us, I observed that the old Japanese cars that had been designed for five persons had officially acquired the capacity for seven. One of them charged past and sprayed muddy water on me. As I stood looking at my soiled cloths in anguish, Tampia proposed we take *Okadas*. These are motorcycle taxis.

There is something about the motorcycle taxi riders of Bamenda – a certain sense of solidarity that cannot be rivalled. They are of all ages, ranging from youths barely weaned from their mothers' breasts to patriarchs that should have been enjoying a peaceful retirement. There are very neat and concerned riders as well as extremely sordid and rude ones, and the sordid ones are often dressed in clothing that seems to have been salvaged from a trash heap. The thing they have in common however is that when they have a passenger, they are always in a mad rush until the passenger is dropped at his or her destination. Another common trend with them is the urge to carry much more than what the motorcycle was built for. Instead of one extra person that the machines were designed to carry, you normally saw two or three – or even four – passengers perched precariously behind the rider.

I was quite surprised when Tampia told me that the motor taxis were the preferred means of transportation to many, especially women. This did not convince me to risk it however, and despite the scarcity of taxis, I insisted we wait for one.

Finally, a yellow cab came with the front seat empty and both of us squeezed in. There was still room in this front seat for a third passenger.

"Where are we going?" I asked as Tampia mentioned some destination to the driver and proposed a hundred francs for each of us.

"We are going to the Bamenda Commercial Avenue, specifically to the NWCA breakfast joint," he replied.

"But I have just had breakfast," I pointed out.

"Yes, but not with Kola Coffee. This place serves Kola Coffee with any snack you want. Connoisseurs like you can have your own coffee, brewed specially. Since you have eaten, you may skip the snacks and just have coffee."

After coffee, we took a stroll along the commercial avenue, up to the Bamenda market area.

"Why do they do business in containers?" I asked. Many shops along this commercial avenue were hosted in metal containers that had been used to bring in goods from abroad. The emptied containers were transformed into offices or shop space, complete with windows and doors.

Tampia laughed at my question. "Some of the owners of the land do not have enough money to construct decent houses, yet they will not sell. The only option therefore is to rent out the space to these container users. However, the municipal authorities are now bent on clearing off all the containers."

We left Commercial Avenue and went through several side streets. There was a proliferation of drinking joints, Pentecostal churches and cacophonic noise. The drinking joints blared music as if they were serving the deaf. The Pentecostal congregations, at all hours, shouted as if God had misplaced his hearing aid. The pastors were louder than thunder. I had always thought that God hears everything, whether whispered, murmured or simply thought. The noise also blasted from shops where pirated music was recorded or electronic equipment sold.

"There is total freedom here," said Tampia. "These are all honest Cameroonians trying to make an honest living and need all the noise to attract as many customers as possible."

"But what of their neighbours?" I asked. "How do their neighbours work or sleep with all this noise, and how do their neighbours enjoy their own music in this confusion?"

"The neighbours do not complain," said Tampia.

"Are you sure?" I asked perplexed.

"It is assumed that everybody enjoys loud good music," Tampia said.

As we moved on, we came across a mad woman dashing from one end of the street to the other with careless abandon. Strangers from Europe would have marvelled at the nonchalance exhibited by the passers-by. Nobody seemed to notice. People went about with their affairs. Farther down the street a madman rummaged through garbage. He had the looks of a Rasta priest and ate whatever he found with relish.

"God drives away flies from tailless cows," Tampia said. "It is virtually impossible to see any of these mad persons sick."

"From the way you talk," I said, "it looks like there are quite a good number of them roaming the streets."

"There are quite a few around and all of them live long."

"Why is nothing done about it?" I asked.

"About their long lives?" Tampia asked. "We cannot just snuff them off simply because they are loony."

"No," I said. "I am not talking about murdering people. It is clear that I am concerned about mad persons roaming the streets."

"Who should do something?" Tampia asked indifferently.

"They do not have families?" I asked.

"Some do," replied Tampia. "But many families, after making attempts to take care of their mad relatives, give up and allow the mad fellows to roam on their own. On the other hand many of them have no families around. Some have been brought in from far off areas and abandoned."

"There are the municipal authorities and the government. You don't have asylums in Bamenda?"

"Not really. What we have here are a few medicine men who claim to be capable of curing madness. Concerned family members often take their demented relatives to them and pay dearly. Some eventually give up when the concern is no longer there and the crazy fellows end up roaming the streets."

After roaming around ourselves for a while, we finally settled into one of the joints for a drink. The neighbours to the left and to the right were selling booze. One of them was a complete shop and sold beer just as an extra, but both of them seemed to be competing with the booze joint we had opted for in terms of roaring music. Our resting spot served assorted beer and many of the customers drank directly from the bottle. In front, by the street side, you had the option of *Soya*, grilled fish, or broiled pork. As we sat drinking, hawkers hovered around selling items ranging from groundnuts and Kola nuts to clothing and footwear. Some lugged assorted electric and electronic equipment, leather belts or countless other items.

Conversation in these drinking joints could be quite interesting. Topics ranging from politics and religion to women and football were handled with the expertise of top class analysts. When I pointed out to the barman that his customers were straining in their efforts to discuss their various topics because of the loud music, he explained that he had to turn up his own so as to beat the noise coming from the musical sets of his neighbours. When I asked whether he was not afraid that the noise might drive away customers, he pointed at the host of customers consuming beer and chatting away with total abandon at the top of their voices.

"I play good music and they like it."

"But you guys could play cool music and that may attract more customers. Don't you see that these guys are here because they have no choice?"

"No!" the barman replied with emphasis. "Loud music attracts them." The loud music, I was made to understand, provides a solution to boozers who want to go home a bit high. With the poverty situation in the country, it is not easy to afford the required amount of bottles of beer that would give satisfaction and give a man the Dutch courage with which to boldly confront a nagging wife. With the loud music, just two bottles of beer are enough to make you soused enough to go home with confidence.

I had already developed a headache as I had to shout each time to get myself heard by the barman. My American accent did not help as I had to repeat myself several times to be understood.

The next day, I insisted on seeing more of Bamenda town. Tampia's uncle again offered one of his vehicles. After some hesitation, Tampia accepted the offer and we drove off.

We visited a few offices where French seemed to be the dominant language and documents on walls or lying around were in French or poorly translated into English.

I asked Tampia why French was so dominant.

'We are just like a captured territory," he said. "In a typical English speaking area, all the organizations with juicy salaries have French speaking Cameroonians managing them. As for documents, it is a normal phenomenon even in government offices and para public organizations. Everything comes in French and is locally translated when necessary, so the end result is usually poor."

"That is strange," I said.

"What is strange about this?" asked Tampia. "We are getting so used to it that it is now done with impunity. Professional translators are packed in all the ministerial departments. Cameroon is one of the countries with a well-recognized professional school for translators and interpreters. Yet documents keep coming to us in French or very poorly translated into English."

"Watch out, Didacus!" Tampia suddenly said to the driver as he swerved to avoid hitting a youth of about ten years, who had been sent to buy beer by some adult. The frightened kid dropped the empty bottle he was taking to enable him get the beer, and it shattered on the hard road surface.

Tampia turned back to me as if what had just happened was a very usual occurrence.

"In all these international organizations in Bamenda," he continued, "English speaking Cameroonians get recruited only when it is imperative that the experts should be English speaking. Even then, some blokes from the French speaking part who have picked up a few words in English still squeeze through. However, where it is difficult to place these French speaking experts, this is compensated by a proliferation of French speaking secretaries, accountants and so on."

"What was that child going to with a beer bottle?" I asked.

"Adults, maybe a parent, an uncle or aunt, or maybe just a neighbour can send the child to procure drinks, drugs or cigarettes. We make full use of our children while they are growing up."

"I hope you are aware that it is not proper for children this young to have access to alcohol, cigarettes and drugs," I pointed out. "This cannot be allowed in America."

"I heard about that somewhere," Tampia said. "But that is because you have spoiled and bad children. Our children

43

do us the favour of running to buy the alcohol and cigarettes but hardly ever dare to smoke or drink until they become adults. Your brats out there grow up wallowing in booze, cigarettes and even hard drugs despite all he caution you take."

Tampia's reasoning had a problem but I could not lay my finger on it. I remained quiet for some time as Didacus drove on.

I noticed that most of the police officers in charge of curbing the chaos at certain very busy points were female.

"This is a big plus for Cameroon," I said "From every indication, there is serious move towards gender balance in the police force. I suppose it is the same with the gendarmerie."

"Why do you say that?" Tampia asked, surprised at my sudden change of topic.

"Look around," I said, "at all the road junctions. There are neatly dressed policewomen."

"Let's stop at one of those road junctions, and you listen to them speak," said Tampia.

He asked the driver to move through Commercial Avenue and slow down at the main market. Then, to City Chemist Roundabout continuing to Veterinary Junction. After going through these places, Tampia no longer needed to explain.

Along Commercial Avenue, around the main gate of the central market, policewomen were ensuring that taxi drivers did not stop to collect passengers without respect for other road users. All of them were speaking French to the drivers, and among themselves, no trace of English.

At city chemist roundabout the policewomen were gathered at the roadside chatting away in French. Some were even using a strange dialect which Tampia told me was from some far off Province.

At veterinary junction where there was some traffic chaos that needed to be sorted out, the policewomen were shouting in French at drivers and motorcycle taxi riders who understood nothing beyond their native dialects and Pidgin English, thus causing more chaos.

"There is no real language for drivers," I said jokingly to Tampia when he asked me whether I had discovered that Cameroon was not treating women from the English speaking side of the country fairly when it came to recruitment into the force.

That night, Tampia insisted that we enjoy life in Bamenda by night.

"Take advantage of the fact that you are here in Bamenda. Have some fun the way Bamenda people do," said Tampia.

"What type of fun can be had here in Bamenda apart from heavy boozing in noisy places?" I asked. "From what I have noticed beer drinking and much noise is the order of the day."

"America is no better," Tampia said. "Each time I watch happenings in America, there is mostly violence even in sports. Have you realized that there is a lot of violence in your own version of football?"

"That is a game for men," I said. "Soccer is now catching up because players have learnt to use a lot of force. Graceful dribbling is no longer the order of the day."

"At least, you agree that apart from booze, we have interesting things like soccer?" Tampia said.

"We have a lot more," I replied. "We have politics, basketball, football, baseball, the circus, the best entertainers and all sorts of interesting pastimes. You can see that here you have virtually nothing. When you are not drinking, you are either in one of those Pentecostal churches listening to some haranguing pastor, or looking for women."

"Just our dances are enough to make any American want to remain here. The graceful Fumbang dance performed by the Kom women, the Makossa and Assiko dances that thrill every nightclub fan and even the bottle dance which is popular in Bamenda are worth any entertainment you can think of."

"So, what are you suggesting?" I asked.

"I want to show you how Bamenda can be interesting by night," Tampia said. "We shall have a drink in Dreamland Cabaret, after which we shall move to One Spirit bar and end up in the Njang nightclub."

"How are we going to move?" I asked rather worried. "I heard something about insecurity at night."

"You are right," Tampia said. "I am aware of that, so we shall get one of my uncle's vehicles. For a small tip, Didacus will not mind taking us around at night."

Our first stop that night was Dreamland Cabaret. The place had class and the music was cool. I commented on the pleasant music.

"When the live band starts playing, you will have more entertainment."

"This place is quite comfortable too."

"The drinks here are pretty expensive," said Tampia, sipping his Kadji beer.

"Is that why the place is not choked with people like in other drinking spots we saw already?" I asked.

"No," answered Tampia. "We are simply too early. Come back a few hours later and you will find the place quite full. The high prices correspond to the quality and class."

"Is this the only one in town?" I asked.

"Actually, there are several, but this one is very popular."

After two hours in Dreamland Cabaret, we moved to One Spirit bar. It was quite crowded and smoking inside was uncontrolled. Young girls dressed to defy the Bamenda cold were hanging around, bent on enjoying themselves to the fullest and maybe rope in a male client for the night. The beer drinking was intense and the noise produced by the DJ deafening. Despite the cacophony that could be labelled as music, the customers of this popular haunt were chatting away as if in some quiet resort.

"Drinking in such places can lead to a piercing headache," I observed.

"Not to the regulars," said Tampia. "There are people who pass their evenings and nights here and only go home towards dawn. Here, the beer is not expensive, there is no protocol and you can do some dancing when you get high. The next day, you can equally boast to your friends that you were out the whole night. Many young bucks get their night's company from here at an affordable price. Meanwhile, visitors to Bamenda can keep busy here instead of passing a lonely night."

"Anyway," I said. "You Cameroonians seem to be quite used to the noise and like it. There is noise in every drinking place."

"The noise is still not at its peak. Come here after midnight and you will get the real thing," Tampia said. "However, not every Cameroonian likes noise. Some are prepared to pay dearly for their relaxation in a quiet atmosphere. If we go to a place called Holiday Resort, you will see what I am talking about."

I wonder whether I enjoyed my stay in One Spirit and was very relieved when we eventually moved on to Njang nightclub. It was after midnight but we still found it rather empty.

"Nightclub fans come in around 2 AM." said Tampia.

Njang nightclub was not bad at all. There was good music, good service, and a good internal arrangement and décor.

The dancing was quite enthralling as each dancer was bent on enjoying himself or herself to the fullest, given the high costs involved here. The young girls were displaying artfully in a bid to attract the idle husbands that had sneaked off from their wives for the night. Other single girls, hookers no doubt, were hanging around the bar, sipping carefully at the beer they had managed to acquire while waiting for some horny fellow to approach. It was virtually like anywhere in the world.

Despite the dim lights, one of the fellows decided I was lonely, good looking and certainly not poor, and came up to invite me for a dance. I assumed that the fact that I was a stranger in the place, not accompanied by a female and concentrated on my booze instead of dancing had made the smart female draw conclusions.

I knew my dancing was not wonderful, but I also knew the female did not seem to care. She was rather thinking of the possibility of making some bucks out of me.

6

On The Way to Kumbo

The next morning we took off for Kumbo, another big town in the Northwest Province. We were jammed in a bus clearly carrying much more than it was built for. Mercifully the road from Bamenda was tarred despite the fact that it was narrow, winding, covered with potholes and quite dangerous. You were always either ascending or descending a steep hill. After a very long decent of a hill with a frightful gradient which I heard was called Sabga, I noticed two buses like our own crawling up the hill while the passengers were sweating it up on foot. Tampia told me they were lucky they did not have to push the buses up the hill.

"If you look carefully, you will see the scrapped remains of many vehicles," Tampia said. "Many people have lost their lives here through ghastly accidents, generally due to brake failure."

After descending the steep Sabga hill, we got to Ndop plane. The road was tarred but full of potholes, an indication of poor work initially and very untimely repairs. The most embarrassing thing however was the nature of the bridges. I am sure that even in other African countries such bridges would not be allowed on such an important road. There were dangerous potholes on the approach to the bridges, and the bridges themselves looked as if they had been designed for footpaths.

"Don't be too surprised about the dangerous appearance of these bridges," Tampia told me. "They were there long before we were born. We grew up to understand that the

49

bridges were constructed by the Germans during the colonial days."

"And they are still in use?" I asked in surprise.

"They have proven to be more solid and lasting than the modern ones constructed these days in parts of Cameroon with all the modern engineering techniques," replied Tampia.

"But they are so narrow," I pointed out. "I am sure many accidents occur here."

"You are right!" replied Tampia simply. "Imagine yourself driving on this road for your first time in the night. You could easily miss the bridge and drop into the stream down below where those terrible rocks are waiting for you to crash-land on them."

I reflected for a while and asked, "Are there no strong politicians from this part of Cameroon, who could exert pressure to have good bridges constructed in the place of these death-traps?"

"Lots of them," Tampia replied. "But they have other priorities. They prefer options that can be easily used as bait to lure the electorate to their side."

"Such an important thing as road safety is not a priority to them?" I could not help asking.

"They personally have nothing to gain from that," replied Tampia. "If you see politicians clamouring for anything, then know there is a lot of personal interest attached to it. The politicians from the areas around these bridges are not powerful enough. The more powerful politicians have their constituency rather far off despite the fact that they cross these bridges before getting there. It is more useful for them to clamour for things right in their areas."

In Ndop, our old bus finally shuddered to a halt. After a thorough examination of the old patient, the doctor, oops, I mean mechanic, decided it had developed some serious engine trouble and would need repairs that might take quite some time. As we sat waiting, admiring Ngoketunjia in its majesty and splendour, I pointed out to Tampia that the hill with a large rock at the crown would be a serious tourist attraction if well-advertised.

"We could go to Bamabalang and admire another formidable feature," Tampia said.

"What would that be?" I asked, thinking of another hill.

"The Bambalang Lake. It is the product of a dam," Tampia replied.

"And what is so particular about this lake?" I asked.

"It has good fish and islands you can visit with a canoe to see other magnificent attractions."

"Is it quite close?" I asked.

"Not really," he replied "But we could go to another tourist attraction ahead and wait for the bus there. That would be the Babungo Chief's palace with an excellent palace museum."

"The museum contains much?" I asked.

"Lots of artefacts," replied Tampia. "There are wonderfully carved items of wood. It would appear the past chiefs were all wonderful craftsmen."

Tampia recommended motorbikes as the fastest means of getting to Babungo to admire the museum items before the bus could be repaired and catch up. To save costs, Tampia insisted that both of us be transported on one bike.

We got to Babungo in less than thirty minutes. After admiring wonderful pieces of art, including a Babungo version of the goddess Shiva, we moved to a bar where we sat waiting for the bus from Ndop.

In a compound not far from where we sat, some sort of celebration was going on which involved lots of eating, drinking, dancing and gun shots.

"That is a *Cry die* ceremony," Tampia explained. "And it may last for several days."

"Days?" I asked "But that would cost a lot of money and time."

"The cost does not really matter," said Tampia. "That is their decent way of seeing off their late ones and the bereaved receive lots of financial and material support from friends and neighbours. The sad thing about it is that such support hardly comes in when it is needed to prevent the person from dying. Friends and relatives instead wait for death before they rally around to sympathise and support." Finally, the bus arrived and our journey continued.

The trip from Babungo to Kumbo was quite rough. We splashed muddy water on pedestrians, some of whom used umbrellas to protect themselves. It was not certain on which side of the road we were moving as the vehicle swerved from one to the other dodging potholes. At another hill called Wainamah where the road was quite narrow, steep and winding, the bus challenged the mechanic's competence again, probably tired of operating as the willing bus being driven to death. After a few splutters of protest, it finally gave up. The driver's assistant quickly jumped down, fetched some big stones and placed them behind the rear wheels. It occurred to me that they were not even sure of their handbrakes. We all had to get down and trek all the way to the top of the hill where we waited for the bus. After a few expert touches with the spanner, and relieved of its excessive human burden, the bus whined up the hill to meet us at more level ground. The rest of the journey was rather uneventful apart from police and gendarme checkpoints. From

Wainamah we had a breath-taking view of Ndop plain stretching to Wasi and Ber in Jakiri, land of raffia palm wine. The large Bambalang Lake, behind the Baminjim dam, was another site worth viewing.

Finally, our tedious journey took us to Kumbo. As we drove up to Kumbo squares, the Catholic cathedral stuck out in the landscape like the statue of liberty at New York Harbour. Behind it was an equally prominent Presbyterian church. Above these churches one could clearly see the popular Banso Baptist Hospital which is one of the best in the country. Across it and disguised behind some exotic trees was the Bishop's house, well designed structures surrounded by beautiful landscape. Tampia told me the Catholics had their own big hospital in a neighbourhood called Shisong which had the best cardiac centre in the country.

There are other things about Kumbo town. It was a centre of culture and tradition for the Nso people. The palace of the paramount traditional leader or *Fon* was located right at the centre of town, with a prominent mosque in front as proof of the wonderful and brotherly coexistence between Nso tradition, Moslems, Roman Catholics, Baptists and Presbyterians. The Israelis and Palestinians could learn much from them.

After booking into Merryland Hotel, we decided to tour the town. Like in Bamenda, there was a proliferation of small drinking spots, small eateries, small businesses and the reckless motorcycle taxis.

"This is a fast developing town," explained Tampia, "with a very hardworking mayor. Everybody calls him a bulldozer."

I liked the climate. It was a lot better than Bamenda. The mayor had struggled and had some roads tarred within the city, so we avoided the muddy ones.

"I read in a tourist guide during my flight to Cameroon about some lake worth visiting around here," I told Tampia.

"That should be lake Oku." he replied. It is a crater lake, very beautiful to look at and located within a forest reserve where there are rare birds, monkeys and exotic flora."

"Are we not going to visit the place?" I asked.

"No," replied Tampia. "Regrettably, it is a bit off from the main ring road and to get there you either go by motorcycle transport if you want to move fast, or you brave a slow ride in an overcrowded car."

"Why don't we hire our own vehicle?" I asked "If we go by what I read in the tourist guide, it is not simply a lake out there, it is a tourist haven."

"Time and funds do not permit us," replied Tampia.

Tampia led me into a makeshift bar where we were served raffia palm wine.

"It is a pity we did not stop in Jakiri which supplies much of this wine to Kumbo," Tampia said. "There you would have had pure unadulterated wine."

The other customers of the place already had large bottles of the white stuff in front of them and drank from plastic cups.

What I enjoyed most in this joint however was the conversation in the Nso dialect. It would appear the people rarely spoke anything else when they were among themselves. Some enlightened looking ones relapsed into English language once in a while but all seemed to have a problem with their pronunciation of certain words.

One old man with stained teeth removed a dirty container from the pocket of an old gown he was wearing and proceeded to apply snuff to his nostrils. As his eyes reddened and glistened with unshed tears, he corked his snuff receptacle well and put it back into his pocket. He transferred his attention to an old raffia bag he was carrying and brought out some reddish nuts. This time, he was generous and offered some to Tampia and myself.

"These are kolanuts," Tampia explained. "Don't bother that they don't look clean enough. They don't carry any bacteria and are good for the heart."

He picked one up and split it into lobes, then, throwing a lobe into his mouth, offered me one. He was already chewing with gusto. Following his example, I dropped the lobe I had been offered into my mouth, but with a lot of misgivings. The kolanut had not been washed and the bag from which it had been brought out as well as the hand that had brought it out were far from clean. Then the taste! As I chewed on the kolanut, I was happy I had only a small lobe in my mouth. The stuff was bitter and tasted awful.

But then Tampia offered me a glass of water and insisted I drink it. Whew! Never had I tasted water so sweet. I guess the bitterness of the kolanut brought it out. What a sensation. I'll never forget that drink of water.

As we came out of the place, I noticed people were taking cover. Then, I understood why. A very large black thing with a mask over its face was making its way down the street. It leaped in the air, hit two sticks it was carrying and kept running. It was full of action despite the fact that it was restrained by some half naked men clinging to ropes attached it.

"That is the *kibaranko*," Tampia whispered to me. "It is the most powerful and the most dangerous juju in Nso land.

"If it is that dangerous," I said, "then they have every reason to restrain it with those stout ropes. What makes it that dangerous? Is it not just a man wearing that huge mask?"

"It is believed that the *kibaranko* is a spirit not a man. How do you imagine that it carries that huge heavy head without feeling it and moves tirelessly all over the place? It could run great distances without stopping."

"A spirit eh?" I asked. "Then how come it is restrained by mere ropes?"

"Those are not ordinary ropes," replied Tampia. "They have been fortified with strong medicine. Besides, once in a while the *kibaranko* succeeds in escaping. At that time it can only be caught by a pregnant woman."

I laughed a bit too loudly and was hastily hushed by a frightened Tampia.

7

From Kumbo to Nkambe

We took off from Kumbo early the next day for Nkambe but opted for a different form of transportation. Bus services were available up to Nkambe and even beyond, but Tampia said that because of the hills that necessitated serious climbing, the buses moved so slowly that it would be a nightmare traveling by them. I discovered later on that the slower journey by bus was far more comfortable than the rough but faster ride by the small cars they called *clando*, and Tampia's real intention was to trick me into a *clando* ride. We thus boarded one of the *clandos* that was competing for passengers at the motor park. *Clandos* were very old cars, mainly Toyotas, reinforced to stand the abuse. Apart from headlamps, these vehicles hardly have any other lights, not even brake lights. Their bodywork is rough with terribly scratched paint. Originally designed to transport maximum five persons, onto just the back seat of these cars are crammed five persons, while another three or four are squeezed onto the front seat alongside the driver. The trunk of the car took close to ten times the amount of cargo it was designed to carry. Using thick rubber ropes to hold things together, the experienced loaders could arrange and pack cargo up to the roof of the car, completely blocking off the rear view. I had opted for the front seat by the door so I could have a clear view of all the beautiful scenery and activities along the way.

"*Clandos* hardly have any documents and are never insured against accidents," Tampia said from behind. "This situation, combined with the fact that they always transport more persons and baggage than is permitted, suits the gendarmes and the police. It gives these forces of law and order the chance to act lawlessly. You would be right if you labelled them, 'forces of lawlessness and disorder'. They encourage the *clando* drivers to transgress all traffic and safety laws, simply for a reward of 500 francs which the drivers give instead of handing over car documents for them to verify."

Tampia wiped his face and continued, "The law enforcement officers write down the registration number of the cars whose drivers have handed over the bank note, an indication that the driver may pass through that checkpoint without being stopped, for the whole day.

As we moved along, we by passed a *clando* with a fifth person sitting in front, to the left of the driver, making it difficult to know who was actually driving the vehicle. There were several police and gendarme checkpoints before we got to Nkambe and at each, the driver jumped out of the vehicle, strode with confidence up to law enforcement officer and offered a bribe of 500 francs. This was readily accepted and these law breaching drivers always took off unmolested and without any waste of time.

At one of these checkpoints, a young man who was transporting his sick mother to the hospital in a very roadworthy BMW car was undergoing rigorous inspection. The gendarme officer meticulously went through his vehicle's documents. Tampia explained to me that the control was so thorough because the young driver was transporting only his mother instead of overloading the vehicle with passengers and giving a tip to the always expectant law enforcement officers. The gendarme officer shouted triumphantly when he finally discovered that the road worthiness certificate of the BMW had expired two days before. He now had a concrete reason to compel the young driver to pay up before he would be allowed to continue. Of course our driver whose vehicle defied all norms of road safety, but who was already prepared to buy his way through, was allowed to go without any disturbance, apart from the fact that his day's income had dropped by 500 francs.

Just before a place known as Kakar Junction, we came across an expressive tea estate. I thought this was great. A lush tea plantation that could compete with any in Sri Lanka, India or any of the great tea producing countries of the far East, was located here in the heart of this remote part of Cameroon.

"Tampia," I said in excitement "this is simply wonderful. Which big company has all this wealth?"

"It is embarrassing to say." replied Tampia.

"Why?" I asked "This is a fortune here. Expansive land all covered with tea. I suppose they do process and package this tea out here too."

"You have said it." Tampia replied. "This tea estate belonged to the biggest state corporation in the country and the second biggest employer in the country after the government."

"I thought I heard you use the past tense." I said. "To whom does it belong now?"

"I wonder whether you will understand what happened except I take quite some time to explain carefully." Tampia said.

"I have all the time." I replied. "The journey is getting boring and your story might make it slightly more interesting" I said.

"Okay," Tampia said. Let us get to Ndu where there will be a stopover. We could have a few private minutes before the journey continues. Walls have ears and you do not know what suspicious ears could be in this car, straining to hear what we are talking about."

I was eager to get to this Ndu. After about thirty minutes we got to a small town where the driver stopped, dropped some passengers and started looking for others to fill the vacated seats.

"This is Ndu town." Tampia told me in response to my enquiring look "Let us move to the side so that I can explain what you are certainly eager to hear."

We moved to the side far enough not to be overheard.

"This tea estate," Tampia said "belonged to a big state corporation called Cameroon Development Corporation, abbreviated as CDC. This corporation owned banana estates, palm estates, rubber estates and tea. There was at least primary transformation of all these products before export. Tea was fully processed and of high quality. The CDC was doing quite well. But then, the massive wealth in the business tempted a few hawks to devise astute means of taking over. It was falsely declared that CDC was in serious trouble and some of its activities had to be privatized. The banana sector was privatized and then, it was the turn of tea. For some reason unknown to Cameroonians only foreigners could buy over the tea sector that was being privatized. It was eventually sold out for less than the tea that had been harvested already pending exportation. All the assets of the tea estates were not accounted for including land, factory buildings and warehouses, equipment and other assets. The irony is that now, less than five years after these scandalous sales, this same CDC is struggling to buy land in this Ndu for the same tea production. To prove that CDC is quite alive and kicking, it is now stretching to other parts of this Province and the South West Province to open the same plantations that had been declared bad business less than five years ago. This same CDC is going back into banana and other plantation crops that had been abandoned at heavy losses to the corporation."

"From what you are saying, it is clear that some greedy pigs intentionally misled the government into selling out good business just for the same persons to rush in and buy at giveaway prices,"

"You have gotten the point, but don't forget that it is top secret

Nkambe was not wonderfully far from Kumbo, but because the road was worse than an abandoned farm to market road, it took three hours to get there. There were places where we waded through pools that could have served as fish ponds. Often, the vehicle got stuck in the mud, and we had to push. Tampia called my attention to the fact that every time we went to push, the women simply took their handbags and strolled ahead to wait for the vehicle where they assumed that pushing would no longer be necessary. Apparently it did not occur to them that as passengers of the vehicle they also had to contribute in the pushing. It was clear that the women felt the hard work belonged to the men.

"Do your women always abandon the hard work of pushing cars to the men?" I asked.

"It is good you noticed it," said Tampia. "When you go back to America, tell all those ignorant feminists who keep ranting about the rights of the woman and how the woman is constantly ill-treated by the man in Cameroon that they are quite wrong. We need to film this scene and show the world how women cheat men in these areas."

"You can't completely dismiss the fact that in Cameroon, it is actually a man's world," I said.

"Maybe," Tampia replied, "but everything the man does here is for the good of the woman. We are the breadwinners and the pillars of the family. We even stretch to the burden of marrying several women, just so we give as many women as possible the opportunity to get married. You may not be aware of this, but marriage is the primary goal in the life of every Cameroonian woman."

"And you still keep girlfriends? I hear it is a common thing."

"It is not only common but necessary," said Tampia. "The unfortunate women who can't have husbands also need a man. At times our generosity provides income to some jobless woman. Finally, you see that everything a man does is to satisfy one woman or another."

"And hurt other women in the process?" I asked.

"In fact, so many women get satisfaction in the process that the few who end up getting hurt do not really matter. That is why many of them accept polygamy and do not take too unkindly to the prospect of their husbands having a girlfriend or concubine."

I saw it would not be easy to make Tampia think otherwise so I decided to change the topic.

"I noticed that virtually all the gendarmes and the police speak French," I said.

"French is the official language to all uniformed men," he replied. "The gendarmes, the police, custom officials, warders and even forest guards all express themselves principally in French. You see, unlike before where a certain quota between English speaking and French speaking Cameroonians was respected, things have gone out of hand now. To get into the forces, which is considered juicy, an English speaking Cameroonian has to have very powerful connections. It is therefore clear that almost all of them are of French speaking origin. The few, who happen to come from our part of Cameroon, pick up this attitude in school and at their job sites, where everything is done in French."

"I thought this country was said to be bilingual, English and French."

"That is the idea but there is very little equality. Besides, with the unequal employment pattern, the police and gendarme and even the public administration are completely dominated by French speaking Cameroonians."

"That cannot be true," I said.

"To prove to you," Tampia said, "we shall visit all the top officials in Nkambe, our next stop. You will see for yourself what I am talking about."

8

Nkambe to Misaje

We arrived in Nkambe early enough to look around and confirm or disprove Tampia's statement that most high officials in the English speaking part of Cameroon were French speaking.

Nkambe is the chief town of the Donga and Mantung Division, one of the main boarder Divisions with Nigeria and there was a prominent customs service in Nkambe to prove it. Most of the towns beyond Nkambe actually shared boundaries with Nigeria and it was easy to simply cross over to Nigeria or smuggle goods into Cameroon as there were very few poorly equipped customs officials, and virtually no frontier police. Given the distance from Bamenda and other parts of Cameroon and with the very bad road connection, much of the items sold here were brought in from Nigeria. Even fuel was supplied from Nigeria.

After Tampia explained all this to me, he sighed and said "It is a pity we shall not be able to see Furu Awa."

"What is Furu Awa?" I asked thinking of some exotic animal or tourist site.

"Furu Awa is one of the sub Divisions in the North West Province." said Tampia. "Because of neglect and abandon, you can only get to it by trekking for days on by a motorcycle ride."

"Why?" I asked, thinking of the considerably shorter time it took us to move from Douala, through several Divisions, despite the constant delays that resulted from Gendarmes and police encounters.

"Just like another sub division, Akwaya in Manyu in the South west Province no specific effort has been made to link these Administrative units to the rest of Cameroon." Tampia said. "This is more than fifty years since independence and to get to these areas, Cameroonians are obliged to go through another country, Nigeria."

"Anyway," I said "This Manyu Divisions is probably out of our safari track. Let us come back to our discussion on Nkambe. You have not given me a reason why you think that a typically Anglophone Nkambe which interacts closely with Anglophone Nigeria should have mainly francophone high government officials running the show. I suppose they also have francophone magistrates and prosecution lawyers even though success in court, and fair and impartial verdicts or decisions, depend on a thorough understanding of the language of the parties concerned."

Tampia smiled. "Let me quote one prominent Nkambe politician. He said 'Since they have not brought us closer to Cameroon by providing good roads, the Government seems to be afraid that we may break off to Nigeria and has thus imposed mainly francophone government officials, including an army battalion to make sure that we don't nurture such thoughts'"

Tampia chuckled and added "and you know what?"

"I am all ears" I replied.

"The whole battalion speaks French." He said indignantly. "In parts of Nkambe town now where many of them have settled, one would think he were in one of those towns in the South Province."

Our first stop was the office of one of the *Commissaires* or Police Superintendents. He received us in French. When Tampia explained to him that I was an American and could

66

not understand French, he frowned and said to me in very bad and heavily accented English, "You should speak French, my friend. It is the most important language in the world."

Well, personally, I had nothing against the French language, although I rather thought that English was more popular. I simply smiled back and promised to get a French teacher.

"One of our local girls could help you out with that," the senior policeman continued. "We call them bedside dictionaries. That is how I have been able to learn English so fast."

"That is very funny," I said, laughing along with the policeman and pretending to enjoy his joke.

From the *commissaire* we moved to the boss of the gendarmes. He told us very rudely in French that he had no time for loafers from America, especially a black one.

The Divisional Officer was more receptive. He had never actually met a black American, as mostly whites were sent to work in Cameroon. Since he became a *sous prefet* as he called it, he had always been posted to very remote areas in the English speaking zone of the country. He was not complaining because out there, he was king. His English was better than the *commissaire's* and he looked a bit neater.

When we were led into the office of the Senior Divisional Officer, he actually came to the door to receive us. I was pleased to notice that among the pile of French language newspapers on the table were a few in English. At last, an English speaking official I thought, but as he continued talking it was easy to make out from his accent that he was of French speaking origin. He explained that his first posting as a Divisional Officer was in the English speaking sector of the country and for eight years, he had continued in that capacity in this part of the country. Even when he was raised to the rank of Senior Divisional Officer, he had remained here, thus he had learned to speak English very well.

Unlike the policemen I had met up till now, the Senior Divisional Officer was dressed in a neat uniform with a clean white T-shirt inside. He looked like somebody who really merited his high office.

After the Divisional office Tampia had a look of satisfaction on his face. His claims about francophone domination were being proved right. However, he still wanted to wipe out any doubts.

"Let's forget about these key administrative staff and try other sectors to prove that this canker stretches everywhere," Tampia said.

Our first choice was the Delegate of Forestry and Wildlife. The guy could not even understand English, let alone, speak it. This was his first appointment in English speaking Cameroon.

I think I have seen enough," I told Tampia. "You win."

After a chilly night in Nkambe, we boarded another *clando* to take us down to Misaje. Misaje was down on the plane, and the decent was quite steep. Because we had left early and Misaje was just an hour's journey from Nkambe, we got to our destination when there was still time for breakfast. I was already used to the rough life, so I did not complain when Tampia took me to a makeshift eating house. It was a small open place with a roof of rusty metallic sheets held in place by sticks. There were no chairs so we perched on some wooden benches and were served a corn flour pancake called *massa* and a porridge also made of corn called *pap*. If those well paid dieticians had passed by, they would have pointed out to us that the meal did not constitute a balanced diet because it was corn and corn. But then, the Italians eat bread

68

and pasta all made from wheat and I am not certain that poor Italians always have enough beef, fish and vegetables to balance the diet. Anyway, we enjoyed our breakfast thoroughly.

9

Journeying From Misaje to Wum

The stretch from Misaje to Wum promised to be an interesting part of the journey. Actually there were no transport vehicles that would go right to Wum, so we settled for another *clando* that would take us to Subum market. From there we could get another one to Wum. This time however, the *clando* was kind of different. It was what they called Toyota Hilux, a relatively high four wheel drive vehicle where passengers competed with luggage on the open carriage behind designed by the Japanese for transporting cargo. Baskets of fowls and a few goats were also part of the cargo. The cabin of the *clando* was reserved for the driver and privileged passengers of some class. These lucky fellows equally did not have a comfortable journey as the driver crammed as many of them into the cabin as he could. When Tampia tried to negotiate for us to have a place in the cabin, he was told we were late and people had booked since the previous evening. The only option was to wait for the next one and it was not clear when it would take off.

As we took off for Subum, I was lucky we were outside of the cabin. It does not mean there was any bit of comfort where we were. We were perched dangerously on sacks of rice and bags of salt, cartons of canned items and frozen fish, bales of second hand clothes, bags of smoked fish and many household items. Tampia told me it was market day in Subum and most of our fellow passengers were traders. A few passengers were going there to buy items like honey, ground nuts, and corn for sale in the big towns.

As I turned round to talk to Tampia, a scrawny ram bleated right in my face. Tampia pushed a basket of noisy fowls away from him, but the jolting vehicle kept bringing the basket back. Some women were sitting very comfortably on top of the assorted cargo and chatting away nonchalantly as if they were riding first class in some luxurious airplane. Two young traders who had opted for the tailboard of the high vehicle did not seem to think there was a possibility of falling overboard. The two of them were actually sleeping. It just shows you how hard life can oblige you to transform any situation into a normal and enjoyable one. Fakirs in India probably learnt their trade through such hard life.

As for me who had been used to comfort all through my life, I thought I would never forget this experience. Then, we passed by a primary school, which I recognized because of an elaborate sign board and children playing outside. The school buildings looked more like barns in a very poor farm. One structure was of mud bricks and thatched with grass. The other structures were also thatched with grass but the walls were simply of mud and raffia bamboos. As Tampia saw me concentrating on this misery, he said, "Such rickety structures have produced ministers and great men."

"All this can be quite unsafe. You can't teach children under such conditions."

"They have no option and even some of the well-constructed schools in big cities collapse once in a while."

I transferred my attention to the children playing outside. I am sure it was break time. Some were actually rolling in the dust, screaming with delight. Others were running around with wheels of bicycles, using sticks to propel and guide them. Some had made toy cars and lorries from the pith of raffia bamboos and were dragging them around with cords. In front of the brick building, a group of girls was clapping their hands in play. The bigger boys were playing football, in their school uniforms and using some cheap plastic ball. Most of the uniforms might have had buttons when they were made, but no longer. Even the shorts worn by the boys were held fast with rope made from the leaves of vegetables or strips of torn old cloth, in place of buttons or belts. All the children were covered with dust from head to toe, and it was doubtful whether they ever washed those uniforms.

I turned to Tampia again, making sure I avoided the noisy ram. "What a miserable life these children are living," I said sadly.

"That may be your opinion," replied Tampia, "but I believe these children are happier than most children in America."

"What rubbish," I said. "Our children have good toys and other wonderful playthings. They even have computer games, cartoons and story books. They have access to the best healthcare, food and snacks. They have all the care you can think of."

Tampia brushed all of this aside saying, "You should add that while your children are pampered by the law and their parents, the ones playing out there are flogged thoroughly at school for the least transgression and frequently receive beatings at home from parents and older siblings. I still believe however they are happier."

"Would you explain instead of just claiming they are happier?"

"These children live quite a free and enjoyable life. Nobody bothers them about regular baths and cleanliness. They may have household chores, but once these are performed, they play till they go to bed. Their beds are simple and do not require clean white sheets and clean pajamas. Simple bread to them tastes like cakes, cookies and choice delicacies that your children no longer even enjoy because they have in abundance. While you are struggling to convince your children to eat and drink all the nice things you provide, these village kids enjoy their food thoroughly even though it is nothing to write home about. They grow up very resistant and hardly fall ill. American children have lots of toys and are now bored by them. On the other hand, these poor children make their own playthings and get full satisfaction out of them. With stiff control and crowded cities, your children have very limited freedom but these urchins can go hunting for birds, rat moles and cane rats. They equally have access to different fruit varieties which they eat without restriction and can equally trespass into farms where they dig and eat raw sweet potatoes and groundnuts or steal sugarcane and other nice things from farms. All this might not mean anything to you since you did not pass through that kind of life but I can assure you that it is wonderful."

I could not quite understand all this but I was sure he had a solid point there.

A sign board announced that we were passing by the Kimbi game reserve. That was interesting. I strained my eyes in an attempt to spot game, which I was certain would be roaming around freely but was totally disappointed. Even the sight of wild birds fluttering around that could have consoled me was totally absent.

"What type of game reserve is this?" I asked Tampia.

"You would be lucky if you saw a few monkeys and birds," he replied.

"Why is it termed a game reserve then?" I asked.

"There were lots of buffalo and antelopes here, not to talk of the assorted species of monkeys," explained Tampia, "but the government was simply satisfied by the fact that it had named it a game reserve. No proper measures were put in place to protect and preserve all the treasure here. I hear some high administrators championed the poaching that went on. The few poorly paid game wardens, without the necessary facilities and logistics, could easily be lured into assisting and abetting poachers

10

Stop Over In Subum

Subum market was quite interesting. It looked like one of those open bazaars that feature in old Arabian Night tales. There were assorted wares and items displayed on the ground. Then, there were huts where you could buy cooked food and drinks, or some other goods. There was lots of fresh milk and sour milk cream, sold by tiny Fulani women, all wearing rubber shoes. In another part of the market were herds of cattle. I was informed that cattle sale was the main reason why this market had developed.

"I am famished," declared Tampia. "Let's have a bite."

He dragged me into one of the huts where we had the option between beans and plantains, beans and some flour balls or *puff puff*, or rice and some liquid stuff of dubious appearance.

"Groundnut soup," the woman announced proudly in response to my questioning look. "Rice and groundnut soup good plenty," she said encouragingly in Pidgin English.

I had spotted grilled meat at a certain angle of the market, so I pleaded with Tampia to get me some.

I noticed two gendarme officers wearing tight and worn out uniforms, moving around the market importantly. Of course they were speaking French, oblivious of the fact that they were operating in a part of Cameroon where the farthest a villager could understand outside of his or her local dialect would be Pidgin English. They were greeted with a lot of respect and Tampia told me that they often ended up with a lot of beer offered to them.

We spent quite some time in Subum, enjoying the soya and Kadji beer. I noticed a group of fellows wearing long robes and gathered over a large bowl of milk. Tampia explained they were Fulani tribesmen sharing a drink of milk. There was a single long spoon for all of them, and it was passed round for everybody to have a drink. My American friends in the health sector would have complained about this but I am sure tuberculosis and other diseases that could be transmitted through this kind of practice did not exist here. The Fulani guys did not seem to care whether teeth and mouths of their fellow participants in this milk drinking party were regularly brushed and washed, or not.

In one of the huts where loud discussion was going on, some elderly blokes seemed to be getting high on some brownish drink.

"The chaps in that hut seem to be getting better fun from the mucky stuff they are having," I pointed out to Tampia "From the looks of things, it must be alcoholic."

"That is *quacha* or corn beer. An alternative to it, also from corn is *nkang* or *sha*," said Tampia "While the men prefer the more potent *quacha*, women prefer *nkang*, especially when it is still fresh."

"You say they are all made from corn? It means they are quite natural. We should have gone for them instead of beer," I said.

"No, no," Tampia shook his head in the negative. "I am not sure you would like the taste."

He pointed to another hut where some old men were having a rollicking time. "What those people are having over there would have been better. It is palm wine."

"Is it what we had in that town where you have this dynamic mayor?" I asked. I could not quite remember the name of the town.

"Kumbo." Tampia seemed to have understood. "It is something like that but this one is from the palm tree itself not raffia. I am not sure you will like this one anyway."

"Why not?" I asked. "I quite enjoyed the stuff from the raffia palm out there in this Kumbo. Is this other palm that different?"

"What you want to drink is fresh palm wine," Tampia replied. "What those village rustics are having is stuff that is virtually artificial. To make ample profit and keep the drinkers satisfied, water, sugar and locally distilled spirit is added to the palm wine before it is sold.

After our swell time in Subum market, we booked for another *clando*, this time a newer version of the Toyota Hilux. I explained to Tampia that I had had enough of the rough time and would prefer a bit of comfort. To convince him further I reminded him of the fact that when I got back to America I would want to remember him positively and that I could really be generous to a good fellow.

"I have direct access to my father's wealth, and he is a very rich man," I pointed out. "And there are good things all over like Western Union and MoneyGram, which enable wealthy guys like us out there in America to remember positive people out here, positively."

Tampia was not a fool and gave a thought to the bribe proposal I was dangling temptingly in front of him.

"Ok," he said. "Just this once. After all we want to get you to Wum in one piece. Don't we? I will book the front seat for two of us only."

This was a seat that was normally occupied by four or five persons.

Getting the driver to reserve the seat for just two of us was not an easy task. The driver had his regular passengers for whom he reserved such seats and he did not want to disappoint them. However, Tampia was used to the game and made an extra financial effort.

When it was departure time, I was happy that I was not one of the passengers in the open carriage behind. There was palm oil and lots of other merchandise that could easily rub off on your body or clothes and leave huge stains. And the number of passengers who shared the open carriage with the merchandise had increased.

Just when we were about to leave, I noticed the driver beckoning at one of the gendarme officers. He was a burly fellow who looked quite sordid in his faded undersized uniform. The chap strode over to the vehicle and started opening the door of the vehicle in a bid to join us in the front seat which we were supposed to have paid for. I held the door tight.

"Laisse la portière," he shouted at me. "Ou je te fais un malheur."

He stuck a huge paw through the window and gripped me by the throat.

"Montre-moi tes papiers," he growled through rotting teeth.

His breath was terrible and I could not help wondering how his wife and girlfriends stood it. Tampia had cautioned me not to talk much, the reason being that though I was a black American and looked very much like any Cameroonian, my accent would easily betray me and I would be treated differently, whereas the idea was to acquaint myself with local realities.

And he was right. My American accent threw the gendarme officer off balance, as I shouted back.

"You have no right here, man. I have paid for these seats, so shove off and find another vehicle, or hop behind and join the other fellows perched on the cargo."

The driver was embarrassed. He had never seen anybody stand up to a gendarme officer so boldly. He was begging Tampia to reason with me. These officers are virtually lords in the area, after the Divisional Officer.

The gendarme officer was also thinking fast. I had an American accent and could have travelled by an embassy vehicle or a private vehicle belonging to an international organization. Now that I was in a normal passenger vehicle, I am sure he concluded I might be on some special mission and exacting his 'rights' at this point as a gendarme officer in the area might likely land him into trouble. He eyed me as if he would wring my neck if we were found in a dark corner just the two of us, and strode off.

"Let's go," I said to the driver who was still trying to convince Tampia to call for the gendarme and let him have the seat he wanted. Faced with a stubborn refusal from me, the driver jumped out of the vehicle and rushed to the disgraced gendarme officer. Although I could not quite hear or understand what he was telling the fellow, it would seem the officer had made up his mind and advised him to take us along.

"The driver is making a fuss over this," Tampia explained, "because he meets these guys on the road every day and he could mobilize his colleagues to task him dearly every time he crosses one of their checkpoints. Again, giving a front seat to a gendarme officer means your vehicle could sail through without any checks or disturbances even if you were ferrying all the hard drugs in the world or your vehicle had no document, or was absolutely unroadworthy.

"Give some more money to the driver to take away his distress," I advised Tampia.

The journey from Subum market to Wum was quite rough. We bypassed the road leading to Lake Nyos, a lake that at one time released very poisonous gas that killed all life around the area, including the inhabitants, cattle, small ruminants, domestic birds and wild life.

The road surface was full of deep eroded gullies and mud. In some parts rocks were scattered or stuck all over the road. The four wheel drive vehicle ploughed on slowly, spurred by the experience of the driver, who knew the road like his fingertips.

11

We Finally Get to Wum

We decided to spend the night in Wum. We would get up the next day and have time to look around before the ride back to Bamenda and the planned stopover at the Menchum falls. There were tourist sites worth visiting in Wum such as Lake Wum and a handful of other crater lakes.

After breakfast the next day, Tampia proposed we go by motorcycle transport to Lake Wum. On our way however, when we were passing by the Wum motor park, we noticed a political rally was going on.

"I would like to witness this," I told Tampia. So we mingled into the crowd of commoners that had been lured to the political rally with promises of drinks and small cash. A small part of the crowd, the true militants of that party, was dressed in party colours and clapped vigorously every time the important looking personalities on the rostrum said anything. The speakers were party bigwigs, most of whom had come in from the capital with heavy wallets and purses. Rubbed in the right direction they could generously spray drinks or dish out cash, after the official part of the occasion.

Not to be left behind, dance groups had turned out in their numbers, waiting anxiously to start performing for the generous party bigwigs.

A tallish guy in bright party colours with a deceptive smile on his face was on the rostrum. An amateur mind reader would have easily discerned that the bloke was not convinced of what he was telling the crowd. The other blighters around did not look any more convincing to me. They all wore roguish smiles and initiated the clapping to make sure that the anticipating crowd gave a very loud encore. TV crews had been brought in from various media houses to make sure the event was viewed in the capital city.

"We must all give total support to the man on top," the tall chap was saying, smiling even more roguishly. "For all the good things he has given us. We have peace, tons of peace, which is rarely found in African countries. Then, there is national unity, development and what have you. Meanwhile, the opposition only makes noise. What can they do for you without any positions in government? When they come to talk to you, they expect you to gather your few hard earned coins to sponsor their trip, lodge and feed them. As for us we stand drinks all around and give envelopes to everybody. Is that not what the people want?"

There was thunderous applause provoked by the speaker's accomplices on the rostrum.

"Then the greatest one of all," continued the inspired speaker, "our man, who has been working for our welfare all this while, leading us away from chaos and poverty, has decided to stay on and continue working for us. Yes, after all these years of sacrifice and selfless service, he deserves a glorious retirement from active service and could have opted to hand over to somebody else and have a well-deserved rest. Yet, we have succeeded in convincing this righteous and most devoted citizen to stay on and save us from fortune hunters. We should all thank God and be grateful he has accepted."

Spurred by the prospect of free beers to come, there was applause from the crowd which a keen observer would have described as not really enthusiastic.

Not being Cameroonian myself, my objective view was that the orator was doing everything to caress the hand that fed him. Praise singing is not a new thing, especially in regimes where all power resides right at the top with the president. After enjoying the rough tourist rides on the worst roads I had ever seen, I was still to see the wonderful things that had descended upon the people of Wum from the highest offices in the country. It was clear that the speaker had been wallowing in abundance and was of the opinion that the desolate crowd in front of him should forget about the misery which was their lot and rather be satisfied with the peace he was alluding to. I am sure he was also considering the pride of belonging to the same Province with the most senior of ministers as a very powerful weapon with which to convince the people that they should be very satisfied.

Other speakers continued and harangued the crowd on the fact that the opposition was now ineffective and dead as opposed to the advantages to be gained behind the ruling party. They did not seem to be aware of the monotony of it all.

Finally, a chap as bald as a coot came up with a sheet of paper, cleared his throat loudly and announced, "As usual we have to keep sending motions of support to our benefactor, especially as he has accepted to stay on as president and save our country from adventurers. If not for him, we would neither be breathing today nor riding in posh cars."

There was a timid murmur from the crowd.

"Yes, posh cars!" he replied, eying the crowd fiercely. "If I own a posh car, then you own it too, because you are my brother. I cannot count how many of you here who have enjoyed a lift in my car. All of us here on this podium have cars and all of you down there have access to them."

Some sighing came from the bold ones in the crowd, an indication that the speaker was not actually telling the truth. One of the poor fellows even went as far as shouting back,

"Have you ever let anybody near your car? Or it is those females that you usually carry around that represent all of us?"

The bold fellow was a government school teacher, I was told later.

"That fellow is taking a great risk," Tampia whispered to me. "It is possible for overzealous gendarmes to pounce on him or for this speaker to compel them to do so."

The speaker looked sternly in the direction where the remark had come from but I am sure he could not make out exactly who the culprit was.

"That young man is lucky that there are very few gendarmes deployed here," Tampia whispered again. "Or he might have fetched himself some serious manhandling from that reckless statement about cars and girlfriends."

Concluding that it was better to ignore the rude interruption, the speaker continued, "We want our head of state to remain at the helm forever. After all, Bongo and Eyadema were there till death. Many others will certainly remain there for life, like Mugabe, Dos Santos, and, well, and others."

The praise singer had certainly run short of ideas. Apparently he had run out of names of chief executives who had stuck to their thrones. I would have helped him with names like Sassou Nguesso or Obiang Nguema if my opinion were sought. I could have reminded him though that Guadafi of Lybia finally got knocked out and Castro on the other hand finally handed over power, although he gave it to his brother. Maybe some of these other chief executives still clinging to power are equally grooming their brothers, or sons.

I wonder whether it occurred to the egghead that he was talking to a crowd of villagers, not to experts on African presidents and their eccentricities, but then, he was earning far more than his daily bread.

Not to leave anything unsaid, the chap continued, "We don't want any half-baked leader to jump in and ruin everything we have achieved. Hurrah for the status quo. So, I am going to read out names of the members of the 'Motion of support' committee. We expect a well worded message, one that will touch our candidate in the heart and make him see that we are all aware of the fact that God created him to rule."

Wow! How George Bush would have loved this. He had been president of the greatest country on earth, but full of ungrateful critics who kept him constantly under fire for each action of his. After only two short terms in office, he was obliged to hand over the baton to mediocre Republicans who ended up being easily beaten by a small inexperienced and unknown black Democrat. Here on the other hand were people accepting every act of their president like the word of God and insisting he should stay on in power forever.

In most countries of today's world, you beg and cajole the people to elect you into any position of power, and competition into top positions is generally keen. But here the opposite was taking place and intelligent persons who would have made competent leaders were publicly proclaiming their incompetence and pleading for the one 'competent' person ordained by God to stay on.

I am sure if you sought for the egghead's opinion about the appropriate presidential term of office, he would have certainly condemned the stupid American policy that presidential term of office should not last longer than eight years, such that others could equally have a chance to enjoy that high office. I am sure he would have recommend that America should rather learn from Cameroon, which had a sound policy of allowing old experienced persons to stay on and use their experience for the benefit of the country. Yes, I am sure the egghead and his important looking colleagues on the rostrum would have all acknowledged the importance of getting the incumbent to stay on in power and they may have a strong point there. Presidents with uncompleted projects like what Bush had going on in Iraq and Afghanistan, could stay on and finish their projects. You see, an American president starts trouble somewhere or ruins the economy, and instead of allowing him to stay on to fix what he had started, the constitution throws him out after eight years and transfers the burden of coping with the stress to a completely new president.

12

More Politics

As the politicians rounded up with their motion of support committee, I pulled at Tampia's arm, an indication that we should shove off.

"You don't want to hang around for the free booze?" he asked

"I thought you had a very bad opinion about these people," I said.

"That is certainly the case," he replied. "But we have all resolved that if the people's money is misused in that way, we should also have our share."

"Your uncle is one of these people," I said "How do the two of you cope with your contrasting opinions?"

"If you look well in our part of the country we all actually have the same problems and the same genuine opinions. But when it comes to speaking them out loud, the opinion of some of us is distorted by the fact that they cannot bite the hand that feeds them by saying the truth. The big party chaps on that rostrum knew that they were misleading the people and did not themselves actually believe in what they were saying."

The lust for money can make certain people go beyond certain limits but this was too far.

I suddenly realized that I was actually witnessing part of what I had come to see. Those Cameroonians who had a bit of common sense had every reason to be disillusioned. Instead of listening on a daily basis to such hogwash, or being obliged to openly deceive the people just because you wanted to maintain your high government position, brave men would prefer to go elsewhere.

We hung on at the rally grounds for a while, after which we decided to take off for Bamenda. I prevailed on Tampia and we hired one of the *clandos* all to ourselves. This time it was a car and slightly more comfortable than the previous ones.

On the way to Bamenda, we had enough time to enjoy the splendour of the Menchum falls. If well harnessed, it could supply electricity to the Northwest Province and relieve the area of the very regular power failures it witnesses on a daily basis. Tampia told me blackouts are as usual as having your daily meals. As we continued on our way, I discovered that some areas of the road were tarred.

Tampia as usual was always ready to explain why.

"The road was among the worst in the country, but because the area was not important enough to receive ample funds for road construction, but votes from the people had to be relied on during elections, it became necessary to do a little deceptive improvement on the road. It was decided that the very bad spots on the road should be paved and drainage provided.

All the way back I kept wondering what good things had been given to the Wum people to deserve a 'motion of support' to the powers that be.

We came across another political rally in a place called Bafut. From their party colours, Tampia could easily make out that it was the principal opposition party of the country.

"They used to pull bigger crowds than this," Tampia informed me. "But now most of the members are disillusioned."

"Why?" I asked.

"They have been dangerously penetrated by the ruling party. Now, nobody knows who is a sincere party leader. While some of the members are defecting to the ruling party, others are more convinced that the English speaking Cameroonians of the Northwest and Southwest Provinces should have their own country."

"Splitting up countries into smaller units is not the best thing. In fact, it is an extreme thing to do," I said.

"They complain of marginalization," Tampia explained.

"The Anglophone Cameroonians should look for better ways of getting their marginalization problem solved," I advised. "They have people high up there in government who certainly have the opportunity of taking it up with the big man."

"That is true," said Tampia sadly. "But the few big Anglophone chaps who manage to penetrate and get close to power are just the wrong ones. The methods they use to get there make them very ineffective as champions of the Anglophone cause. None of them is prepared to take the risk or the time to point out shortcomings in the system or fight for fairer treatment of Anglophones and ordinary citizens in general for that matter. They are more prepared to pick up the crumbs, fill their pockets and chant alleluia to the system."

"You mean when an Anglophone is made minister, he is more interested in his ministerial advantages than using that position to follow the Anglophone cause?" I asked

"He no longer even believes that there is such a thing like an Anglophone cause. With his pockets bulging full of tax payers' money, he forgets about everything else but his family and his big boss."

At the rally grounds, I noticed that there were fewer traditional dances. Tampia informed me that dance groups had always been present whenever the opposition had their rally, but now the numbers have dwindled considerably as the opposition is not capable of rewarding them with weighty envelopes the way the ruling party does. It has become a commercial world, so patriotism is no longer the key word.

The speaker, a bearded chump with a husky voice, was ranting about the evil ways of the ruling party.

"They are more deceitful than the devil himself," he was saying. "Look around you and ask yourself what we need most. We need schools, hospitals, pipe borne water, industries and most of all roads. Do we have these things?"

"No!" the crowd roared back. I would have joined that crowd myself if I had been a Cameroonian. The desolation I had seen as I moved round the Province stuck out like a sore thumb.

However I noted something important. There was a high level of political tolerance in Cameroon. When I mentioned this to Tampia, he accepted.

"The bloke ranting out there can speak freely, hurl abuses at the regime and the president, and yet go unmolested. For that, even the most stubborn opposition party leaders would accept that there is some progress."

Our attention was diverted to the bearded orator as he continued. "I agree with you. We have struggled to have these things from the government but in vain."

There was derisive laughter all around.

"Yes," continued the speaker, encouraged. "Let the government know that we want development, roads, good schools and so on. We don't need ministers because instead of bringing development they rather ensure that elections are not fairly conducted."

The applause was really thunderous for such a small crowd.

Politicians! I thought. The extremes to which they can go are never limited. A minister is for the whole country and not for a particular area. Cameroon is a poor country, well known for football no doubt, but not rich enough to throw wealth around the way the fellows of the opposition always expect. The way the bearded guy was speaking, one would have thought that Cameroon was not a poor country but one of those rich developed countries that could easily afford tarred roads all over, hospitals in every village, universities in every town and water flowing everywhere. I had never been to any African country before, but my friends who had travelled had given me dreary pictures of the African landscape. I had been shocked all along at my experiences in the Northwest Province of Cameroon, but I was coming from a developed world and the sharp contrast was bound to cloud my eyes.

Tampia suddenly took me back to reality. "That speaker is right. The national cake is not shared out fairly each year."

13

Bamenda Again

Back in Bamenda, as I sat in the dark with Tampia's honourable uncle, I was still wondering what assessment to make about the trip. As we sat lamenting the blackout, which set in at a particularly intriguing moment of a show we were watching on TV, Tampia reminded me that many of the towns we had passed through were linked to the national electricity grid, yet, the business places were using their small generators every night. He went ahead to explain that electricity supply was an uncertain commodity in the Province and could fail at any time. You were grateful when a full day passed without blackouts, and these often came without prior notice. Tampia equally pointed out that most of the political elite live out of the area and would not bother to take up the point with the higher authorities. The population of the Province had thus decided to cope with the little they could get.

We were very grateful when just after fifteen minutes of darkness the lights came on, although we were aware of the fact that darkness could resurface again at any time and many more times.

"How was your trip?" enquired the honourable gentleman. "I hope you saw all the beautiful sites of tourist attraction, the smiling, welcoming and satisfied people, the beautiful landscape and all the good things."

"There was good beer and girls who smiled at me to get a buck from me, but not everything I saw was good," I replied frankly.

"Oh!" he exclaimed. "I hope you did not run into some of those hopeless opposition leaders who would not spare anything to spoil the image of our country and president."

"Not really," I replied "Would you imagine that all the gendarme officers I met spoke French. Most of the Senior Divisional Officers and Divisional Officers are Francophone?"

"Ah that!" replied Tampia's uncle. "That is national integration for you. Go to the francophone zones and you will meet Anglophones who hold high offices."

"But uncle," Tampia stepped in, "it is clear that each time, if one thousand gendarmes or police are recruited, less than fifty of them are Anglophones. Out of all the Senior Divisional Officers and Divisional Officers, Anglophones constitute less than…"

The Member of Parliament looked dangerously at his nephew. "These are state issues and the president knows best," he shouted. "Who are you to challenge him? If French speaking Cameroonians are better administrators and fairer law officers, then they should be the ones to be recruited and appointed into administrative positions. After all, in those big schools in Yaounde, they teach in French and everything is done in French, a language that our francophone brothers understand better. Don't you see that where we are good, Anglophones are given the posts of responsibility? For example, in the Northwest and Southwest Provinces, we have Anglophone principals in most schools and all our members of parliament like me are Anglophones. We even have Anglophone magistrates in our courts this way. I don't know why minority peoples are always whining about marginalization and are so sensitive that they see shadows in every honest act by the legitimate government that should understandably come from the majority. Minorities are small and should accept the role of little brother which automatically goes with access to a smaller piece of the national cake. All fingers are not the same. We Anglophones are quite well treated in Cameroon but we keep threatening national unity."

I could have clapped at this rhetoric, but since I did not know how the honourable gentleman would take it, I decided to keep quiet.

The next day, the honourable MP took me along to a youth meeting where he had been invited as one of the speakers. It would appear the president of the country had developed an excellent youth policy, aimed at encouraging youth in every possible manner to become responsible and productive Cameroonians. The guest speakers however opened the meeting haranguing the youth for being lazy and making the excellent presidential polies unproductive. One hurled, "You all lack initiative and would be only too happy to depend entirely on the government for a livelihood." Another made allusions to the fact that Nigerians had moved in and now control the Bamenda market and lots of businesses, while lazy Cameroonian children complain about unemployment. One stern looking speaker urged the children to take their cutlasses and hoes and go to the farm because school certificates will never put food and drinks on their tables.

When it was time for the youths to talk, I discovered them to be as smart and full of initiative as any American or European. Quick reasoning pointed fingers at the elders who seemed to be blocking the progress of the youth.

The first juvenile speaker gave fire back for fire. "All of you who have just spoken are above sixty-five years of age from every indication, yet you are still clinging to high positions. There is the governor there, two ministers, three general managers of government corporations and two members of parliament. If you stick to these positions, where do the youth fit in? During our civics classes in primary school, some of your names figured in our notes. Today, close to twenty-five years after, you are still there. Maybe, according to you, the youths are supposed to remain under your weight all our lives. How do you then expect us to grow and become as successful as you?

"You are big men and can send your children to any university abroad, after which they have the choice between staying on out there or coming back to Cameroon for you to fit them into the few juicy spaces left over from your persistence in power. Those of you who prefer to keep their children back in the country use your connections and wealth to get them into our professional schools from which they are sure to land good jobs. Which of you sitting up there has ever thought of sending his son or daughter back to the farm or to the Bamenda market to sell provisions? All we the youth are asking for is the opportunity to compete fairly for all opportunities in Cameroon. If we fail at that level, then blame us for not working hard."

There was thunderous applause from the youths as he sat down and another fire spitting youth jumped up.

"Among the youth sitting here," he said "many have university degrees to prove they have not been sleeping. Others may not have any academic qualification through no fault of their own. Now if you gentlemen sitting up there are capable of providing capital for your sons to start a good business, most of us come from poor parents who barely managed to send us to school. You don't expect us to steal in order to start a business. One of you mentioned the Nigerians that have flooded the market. Who allowed them to do that, is it not you, our parents? Nigerians penetrated the Bamenda business horizon long before we were born and are now simply handing over to their children."

Then a girl stood up.

"You are like our fathers, giving us advice," she said to the guest speakers. "Yet, instead of advice, you are dishing out invectives. We were in school with some of your kids, and they are now out of the country, in high government professional schools or in high positions. I have been unemployed for five years since I left university and I have junior siblings to take care of. When you carelessly talk of going to the farm, to some of us who grew up in Bamenda town and whose parents have no land to cede, where do you expect us to get land? How do you expect somebody like me who has been unemployed for so many years to have money for inputs?"

From the hot speeches packed with venom and rhetoric, it was clear the youth had much pent up anger and frustration. I am sure my honourable host and his peers wondered why such a meeting was ever organized and regretted attending.

On the way home, I was witness to a strange and troubling scene. A cow was being taken for slaughter and was led by a very stout rope by a man. He had an assistant behind holding another rope that was tied to the cow's leg. This other rope enabled the assistant to pull back the cow whenever the angry animal attempted to charge and knock down the fellow that was pulling it in front. The cow was showing every sign that it understood where it was being led to and its angry tantrums scared every passer-by. I wondered if I would feel like that cow sometimes if I were growing up in Cameroon.

When the thoughts of the cow left my mind, I noticed one of those noisy bars where loud music and conversations at high tones compete with each other. The usual *soya*, fish and grilled pork were available and happy revellers were having a swell time.

"Let's stop here for a drink," I proposed.

"You can't." protested Tampia's uncle. "That is a run down and very noisy place. How would you perch on those benches?"

"My trip round the Province has taught me a lot," I replied. "I have learnt to take life as it comes and enjoy everything life offers me."

"But we have assorted drinks in the house. You can have your choice and drink in comfort," the honourable gentleman said. "If on the other hand you prefer to drink out, I have much money and we could have a drink in any posh and respectable place in town."

"There is always time for that," I replied. "But for now I am sure I will enjoy this place."

Reluctantly, the parliamentarian asked his driver to park by the bar. As we entered, several blokes who recognized Tampia's uncle jumped up from their seats and greeted us very respectfully. Those who were wearing hats doffed them in respect for the honourable man. Hastily, seats were liberated and offered to us by smiling and expectant revellers.

I was later informed by Tampia that his uncle's main reluctance to sit in that bar stemmed from the fact that he would be expected to stand a round of drinks to those fellows who were greeting so effusively. As a man elected by the people, taking a drink in a public place meant showing the people that you were with them, and the only such language the people understood was being part of a generous round of drinks. In Bamenda, everybody expected drinks from the parliamentarian; few ever thought of offering one to him.

As we settled and were served with our choice of drinks, I was marvelled by the different types of beer lined up on the shelves. I could identify more than twenty brands of lager and stouts.

I decided to concentrate on the conversation that characterizes such drinking spots. One bald fellow, whose head was smoother than the bottle from which he was drinking, was bent on passing through his point.

"The people of this country will never be satisfied, even if you do your best to guarantee a democratic succession," he was saying.

"And what do you mean by that?" asked a fellow with a goatee who was chewing with much appetite on a piece of *kanda*. The skin from slaughtered cows hardly serves for the production of leather these days in Bamenda. People transform it into a snack sold in bars or served with certain traditional dishes.

"Our president has acted unlike his colleagues in other African countries who are creating dynasties."

"I remember that only Morocco and Swaziland have dynasties now. Ethiopia is no longer an empire and Bokassa's attempt to create one met with dismal failure," the *kanda* eater said.

"You forget that in Togo, DR Congo and Gabon, sons have succeeded in inheriting power from their fathers. I suspect that the president in Brazzaville is grooming his own heir," said the bald speaker.

"If that is what you mean," said another reveller, "it does not happen only in Africa. Power passed from Ali Bhutto to his daughter Benazi, even though she was a woman, and Pakistan is an Islamic country where women are much marginalized. Now, within her political party, power has somehow moved to her son, although he is still a kid."

"That is it," said another speaker. "Very glaring just like in India where the Ghandi family kept ruling. Many African presidents on the other hand rule and die without any intention of imposing a son on the country despite the fact that they have able sons, old enough to rule. Yet you chaps always wrongfully suspect their intentions. African presidents are so loved and respected that much of the positive aura rubs off to their sons. They no longer need to impose them on the people, but when these great leaders die, their followers get so enamoured with the son such that they insist on making him the new leader."

I could notice that our Parliamentarian was straining to get every bit of the conversation but pretending to be aloof.

A thin fellow with a hungry look was speaking now.

"If a president's son is smart enough to enamour all the old party bigwigs into guiding him into power, then the praises go to the young man and not to the expired president," he said.

"You are wrong there," said a chunky guy with a large bottle of Guinness stout. "Praises should rather go to the old man whose position as president brought the son into the limelight. What degree of smartness is needed? A president simply needs to instruct that his son be made president after him and all his stooges will comply, even though they may be hungry for power themselves."

"So you all see that smart presidents simply leave the position of a successor open, but make sure that in his absence, you replace him with his son and convince the whole world that it is the people's wish," said one of the first speakers.

"But these children have to be groomed for power if their father intends to hand over to them," said a young man who had just finished wolfing up a plate of *soya*. "You don't want an incompetent heir. They should normally be made ministers and things like that before the time comes for them to become president."

"But people will raise eyebrows if a president openly makes his son minister," commented one of the revellers.

"That is why some of the presidents start by pushing their sons into big business," said another.

"There is still the risk of being heavily criticized if a president gives much money to his son to do business. People will start questioning where all that wealth is from. I think it is safer to bring a son into the limelight through the position of minister," said the Guinness drinker.

"Anyway," continued the Guinness drinker after a short pause, "talking about succession is a distasteful topic to African presidents, who always have the tendency of clinging to power and want to remain there forever."

"That is the tendency actually," replied another boozer. "But initially, African presidents always determined clearly who would succeed them if something happened suddenly. Houphouet Boigny, Kenyata, Nyerere, Kaunda and Ahidjo all accepted the fact that power should go to someone else if they decided to retire or suddenly die. That is why they openly appointed a prime minister or vice president and gave him the constitutional right to succeed if something suddenly happened. Today, however, most presidents want to give it to a brother or a son and since they are afraid to do it openly by making their favourite a vice president or a prime minister, they leave the succession issue cloudy.

"You are right," said another reveller.

"There is a genuine reason for this change," the Guinness drinker pointed out. "An established heir can easily arrange to snuff out the life of the president and step in."

"That may not be the real reason, though, why presidents no longer appoint an heir apparent," said a Kadji beer drinker. There seemed to be many Kadji beer drinkers.

"Have you blokes not realized that it is more democratic to have elections after the death of a president rather than a simple successor?" said yet another Kadji beer drinker.

Kadji beer seemed to be a very popular brand

"Our African presidents," he continued, "guarantee democratic succession by arranging for the constitutional process of free elections after their demise. This is better than father to son directly."

"Like Bush to Bush?" asked another bloke.

"Bush the son was not put there by his father. He worked hard to get there," said the Guinness drinker.

"That is true," said a Kadji beer drinker, "but in Africa it is the same. No president has actually made his brother or son an heir. You see that we are better than Cuba where Castro simply handed over to his brother?"

"Cuba is a special case," said the Guinness drinker. "On the other hand, some presidents in Africa now tacitly prepare their sons for power and tactfully eliminate the position of a constitutional heir like you have vice presidents in America or Nigeria, since it would be scandalous to position their sons in this position of a constitutional heir. However, to guarantee that their sons succeed, they appoint a stooge into a position where he can conduct elections and rig to push in the president's favourite, be it a son or brother. The president never announces his choice openly but whispers into the ears of those who can work for its success. On the other hand, if the president's son is smart enough he might impose himself through his father's stooges."

"But is it not more democratic than simply handing over to an appointed heir? Don't forget that we are now in a multi-party system." said yet another Kadji beer drinker.

"I don't quite understand what you mean by constitutional heir in situations where we don't have monarchies," said one of the boozers. "How does somebody become president in a democratic system without being elected?"

"In America, it is quite clear that a president is elected on a party ticket. If he dies halfway or resigns, some constitutional replacement takes over and continues to the end of the term of office before fresh elections are held. Generally, it is a vice president who takes over and completes the term of office. It is the same in all great democracies, even in neighbouring Nigeria," said our popular Guinness drinker. "In small undemocratic central African countries, presidents find it tricky to openly place their sons in such positions like vice president of the country and heir apparent. That is why they give constitutional power of taking over to a stooge, such as the speaker of the House, and give him a very short period over which to organize fresh elections. To ensure that this stooge does not grow horns, he is constitutionally blocked from running for post of president himself and made to understand that he is placed there to enable the president's son or favourite to succeed in getting elected. It is quite simple. You don't allow any gap otherwise some other powerful person might come in and stick."

"That must be true," said one of the revellers. "With a bit of rigging and a lot of cash to throw around, it is always certain that the president's choice will be shoved in easily."

"But not all sons of presidents are ambitious to rule," said a Kadji beer drinker who had been quiet all along. "If a son is given ample capital and all the openings and opportunities to do lucrative business, he may prefer to avoid the stress and headaches of politics, and rather go for *la dulce vita*."

With that I looked up to see that Tampia and his uncle were already headed for the car. With a head full of conversation, I followed them.

Our next visit was to the home of another politician. This one had his own political party consisting of his family and a few close dependants. From every indication, his political party consisted of less than fifty militants, but this pompous politician had the air of Napoleon riding into Paris during his triumphant return from Elba. He ridiculed with disdain the leader of the principal opposition party who had millions of militants, a sign that he was really a great leader with a great following. Instead of talking about his political party he was rather heaping praises on the regime as if he were a militant of the ruling party. Tampia later on explained to me that the old chap got all that arrogance and pride because he considered himself a member of the presidential majority.

"How is that?" I asked.

"You see, some smart fellows have created parties that have no following and so support the president and his party in everything and in every way. This gives them the chance to relax and subsist on the small benefits they reap from giving unequivocal support to the regime during elections and other issues."

"From what I understand, their numbers are totally insignificant. Do they have anything to add to the success of the ruling party?" I asked.

"They are most certainly lightweights," replied Tampia. "But there is always much money to throw around during elections and these smart hawks grab what they can. The ruling party does not spare a dime when it wants to win."

14

The Land of Afo-Akom

That evening Tampia proposed a trip to the land of Afo-akom.

"And what is that?" I asked.

"It's an old piece of art, a carved statue of wood," replied Tampia. "But this one is not ordinary. It was actually carved by Yuh I, one of the prominent rulers of the Kom tribe who presented it to the people of Kom as their guardian. Fon Yuh I also carved two females as wives to the Afo-akom and made sure he provided the Afo-akom a prominent penis to ensure it satisfied these females thoroughly."

"Hmm… sounds interesting. We saw many wonderful wooden pieces of art in Babungo and other places. There are even some here in your uncle's house," I said "What is so very special about this one?"

"It is supposed to have supernatural powers and is the keeper of the people of the great Kom tribe," replied Tampia.

"Is it?" I asked in disbelief.

"Yeah, but it was some local criminal that made it known all over Cameroon."

"What?"

"It was stolen by this native and taken to Bamenda where it was sold for a mere pittance. The fellow who bought it took it down to Douala where a connoisseur bought it for a far bigger sum and took it across to America, where it probably fetched several hundred thousand dollars. The Kom people claim that while in the museum in America, this piece of art from Kom was the masterpiece."

"How did it get back to its place of origin?" I asked.

"It is alleged that some missionary fellow who had preached in Kom for long, and knew about the disappearance of the invaluable masterpiece and its importance to the Kom people, discovered it in the museum in America," replied Tampia. "Through diplomatic negotiations it was returned to Cameroon and had a state reception."

"I am sure I would like to see it when we go down to this place," I said.

"You won't," replied Tampia simply.

"But why?" I asked, surprised. "Such a masterpiece should be well displayed. It would be a real tourist attraction."

"On the contrary," said Tampia. "The Kom tradition does not allow it to be seen carelessly. It is kept away from everybody and only displayed briefly for a few hours each year."

"What a waste," I said sadly. "I suppose the carved statues that serve as wives are also kept away from the public"

"They are also kept away."

"What a waste," I said. "Such a tourist potential kept away just like that."

"It was not meant for fundraising," said Tampia. "The Afo-akom was made and given to the people of Kom for a specific purpose, and the people are respecting it."

The next day we were offered one of the vehicles of Tampia's honourable uncle for our ride to Kom. Even Tampia seemed to have had enough of the rough rides in *clandos* and happily went along with the generous offer.

The journey was no different from previous ones. For a distance of about ninety kilometres we came across seven checkpoints manned by gendarmes, all speaking French of course in a typically English speaking part of the country. The

110

numerous checkpoints as I had learnt hardly ever apprehended criminals or defaulters although most of the vehicles that plied the road had irregular documents, and many banned or unlawful items such as marijuana and poached animals were transported in them. Five hundred francs was the fee to convince the gendarmes to look the other way. The gendarmes thus always went home with their pockets full.

Along the road, I noticed a well-constructed polytechnique. Tampia informed me that it was as good as any institution of higher learning in America. As we passed a prominent seminary for Catholic priests, I noticed that the signpost announcing it was in French. 'Seminaire Saint Paul', it read, despite the fact that it would have been more appropriate in English.

"The priests here are all French speaking?" I asked Tampia.

"Actually," said Tampia, "after road construction, the contract for road signs was given to a Francophone, despite the fact that the road is located in the heart of Anglophone Cameroon. In a bid to finish his work quickly and rush back to his Francophone home town, the contractor had not even bothered to visit places like the seminary that constituted important landmarks along the road and qualified to have signposts named after them. After hastily gathering information as to the fact that the institution was a seminary and named after Saint Paul, the blighter would not even have the common sense to consult knowledgeable Anglophones in the area and get the right thing in writing. Neither did he even stop to consider the fact that he was operating in Anglophone territory and road signs should be in the English language."

I thought Tampia was through but he seemed to have remembered something else.

"We will still come across some of these eyesores that drive Anglophone Cameroonians into desperation. A glaring one is the Saint Bedes College in a village called Ashing, one of the most prominent educational institutions in Anglophone Cameroon. The signpost there simply reads 'Collège Ashing.' Because the French word almost looks the same as in English, one could guess that this important landmark is a college, but which one?"

As we rolled along in the car in what was one of the most comfortable rides I had experienced in Cameroon, I thought back to my history classes and discussions of 'divide and rule'. I found it interesting how Cameroonians fight over Anglophone and francophone representativeness and whether 'Saint Bedes' is maintained or not in referencing a school named after him or her in the middle of Cameroon. Even if Saint Bedes were included on the signpost, how many people actually know something about this Christian saint, and how much was the saint's life linked up with everyday life and death in Cameroon?

The vehicle slowed down as we approached a herd of cattle moving on the main road. There could have been close to a hundred cows. The cowboys waved their sticks and hit some of the cows mercilessly to get them out of the way for us to pass. As the journey continued, we by passed other herds. It was quite a risky affair as the cows looked quite wild and their long horns came close to the windows of the car as we by passed them.

"Where are all these cows being taken to?" I asked Tampia whom I had mercilessly bombarded with questions since my arrival in his country. He responded each time graciously with knowledge and pride.

"They are coming from cattle markets in Boyo Division where we are going," he answered "And they are being taken to the big cattle market in Bamenda. From there, some of these cows will continue on a journey of no return to the coastal areas."

"There is no other form of transporting them?" I asked.

"There are no trains this way," he answered. "And taking them down by lorry is quite expensive. The cattle traders find it cheaper to hire these cowboys to move them from market to market while the traders themselves move by vehicle."

"I wonder... they are not stolen along the way? Don't you have cattle rustlers here?"

"Quite a few," Tampia answered. "But rustling takes place mostly at the level of the grazing lands. It is believed that these cowboys who lead the cattle herds to the market have very strong medicine to protect them."

After passing through an abandoned toll gate, we came to some well-constructed houses abandoned in the bush. Vandals had had a field day with the roofing sheets. Apart from a signpost showing that this property belonged to the police, there was no sign of life around.

"How did it come about that these buildings were constructed and abandoned here?" I enquired.

They were constructed during the period when this road was constructed," said Tampia. "They were used as lodgings for the families of the expatriate staff of the road construction company, including recreational facilities and warehouses for certain valuable equipment. Afterwards, they handed these facilities to the government of Cameroon and left. The local council could have put them into good use if allowed. For a long time no decision could come from Yaounde as to what use could be made of the structures. It is close to twenty years now, and the facility is still abandoned to wild animals, vandals and the bush."

Why would a poor country like Cameroon abandon such valuable property to rot away like this?" I enquired.

"These are problems of a centralized system," Tampia readily answered. "All decisions must come from Yaounde, even for small things such as this one. If you investigate well, you will discover that several commissions have been set up, to come out with a decision on what to do with these buildings. Each commission has spent a fortune, visiting the place and holding useless meetings just to end up with a report that would be discarded, and eventually another commission is set up," explained Tampia sadly. "When the road construction company completed their work and left, these buildings were all intact. They could have been handed over to the municipal authority of the area to make good use of them. Instead, they waited for years and finally claimed it was police property, and I am sure they will never be able to make up their minds as to what use to put it."

"What a waste," I said and remembered vaguely that I had made this same statement several times before.

"You have not seen anything," continued Tampia. "Go to Gwofon and other parts of this Province and you will see beautiful structures that have been abandoned to rot in the bush. What a bad way to manage a country."

"I did not know where this Gwofon was, but I agreed with him.

"Look at the case of Santa," continued Tampia. "The town where we stopped on our way from Douala to Bamenda."

I nodded.

"I am sure you will never forget the frustration we had when all the public stand taps produced no water."

I remembered clearly how more than twenty-five thousand persons were saddled with serious water shortage because their water sources were located in a Government eucalyptus forest, when it only needed a small signature from the pen of the minister for the problem to be solved. The minister had not stayed completely aloof to the problem when it was reported to him. I learned from Tampia after my return to the States, that he had sent experts in forestry to visit the place, but the small signature took about a year to come, although it had been clearly established that eucalyptus trees were the cause of the problem.

"You see," said Tampia, "the decision must come from Yaounde, and nobody cares out there about these abandoned buildings in a system clogged with bureaucracy.

"Many other areas have the same problem that Santa is facing but nobody in Yaounde seems to understand the urgency of the problem and the fact that thousands of families are suffering." Tampia sounded very bitter.

The road started winding. We were moving into an area full of hills and valleys. Mercifully, it was tarred, and I started wondering out loud how people travelled on this road before it was tarred.

"For this distance of about ninety kilometres, it usually took a whole day to travel it during the rainy season," Tampia explained, as we passed the great Mbingo Baptist Hospital. Together with the Njinikom Catholic Hospital, the area is fully guaranteed of improved medical attention. I realized that the role of the missionaries in medical health care was quite prominent.

We arrived in Belo and the town was bustling with population and activity. We learned it was market day.

"This is not like the Subum cattle market," Tampia explained. "It should be interesting though to stop for a short while so you witness a real market day."

"That will be nice," I said.

"Besides," said Tampia, "this town too is reputed to have a very dynamic mayor, just like the one in Kumbo."

"So apart from these two in the Province," I asked, "all the others are nothing to write home about?"

"Not quite that," Tampia replied. "There are some who are quite bad, either from total ignorance of their roles and responsibilities or from the fact that they struggled to become mayors simply to fill their pockets with as much money as they can grab. Again, some are simply lazy, while others lack initiative. Then there are a few good ones but the mayor here and the one in Kumbo somehow excel."

The driver parked the car in front of a line of booze joints which were all full even at that early hour. As we moved up to the main market itself, the crowds grew thicker. Just like in the Subum market, medicinal plants, household items, electronics, and used clothing were displayed all over on the ground. At the main market itself were makeshift and permanent stalls where you could buy just anything you needed, new or old.

You could buy every food item transformed from local farm products. At one angle you could buy goats, sheep and chicken. Some buyers from Bamenda were sweeping off all the plantains and unripe bananas to be carted to markets in Bamenda. Two vehicles with loudspeakers were parked not far from each other, using loud music and announcements to advertise whatever they were selling. I think one was selling some traditional liquid medicine. Not to be left behind, hawkers were shouting at the top of their voices in a bid to attract buyers. If you preferred local liquor, you could have your pick. Everybody was busy.

Tampia proposed we sit down for a drink.

"You see," he said, once we selected and settled into a joint, "the intention behind market days is not only coming to buy or sell. The real pleasure is derived from these intense human interactions as well as the joy of relaxation in one of these bars."

I lifted my beer in a toast to Tampia and said, "I must admit I have become accustomed to the noise, and I do enjoy watching all the eccentricities of market day from here with someone like you. It's like theatre for the price of a beer, no?"

Tampia pointed at a mad man, "There is proof of what I was just saying. No mad man or woman in these areas misses market day. Some trek for distances just to be part of this ambiance."

When we finally got to Fundong, the capital of Boyo Division, we stopped for a drink. I was surprised to see Tampia buy a crate of beer, two bottles of whiskey and some cigarettes.

"To visit the palace," he explained, "you take along some whiskey and cigarettes for the *Fon*, then you add beer for his courtiers."

"You are talking about the chief. Why do you call him 'Fon'?" I asked.

"*Fon* is a distinguished title for great traditional rulers or chiefs in the Northwest Province. It means he is not a simple chief."

"What of the other chiefs?" I asked.

"Today," replied Tampia, "every small chief wants to be called 'Fon', and would take umbrage if you don't address him as thus."

After a very steep climb of close to 30 minutes, we got to the palace of the *Fon* of Kom.

"Why does he live so far from his people?" I asked.

"Oral tradition has it that the people migrated from a place called Babessi, led by a woman, and following the trail of a boa constrictor. The trail disappeared in this place known as Laikom, so the palace was located here. The other people wandered around and looked for appropriate places to settle. The brave Kom warriors chased other tribes away and settled farther and farther away from the palace."

"I can see it is quite a big place, but many of the huts seem to be empty."

"The past *Fons* used to have as many as a hundred wives, and these buildings were there to accommodate them," said Tampia "Now, the *Fons* have fewer wives and the old ones are dying off."

Tampia arranged for us to penetrate into the inner court with our shoes on and advised me to take off my cap as only titled men were allowed in the *Fon*'s presence with caps or hats on. The inner court was an impressive open area paved with cobblestones. We went in, in single file and bent low as we passed in front of the smiling *Fon*. After placing our gifts before him, we were shown where to sit. I noticed that the *Fon* was not spoken to directly but through some kind of interpreter, even when you were speaking in the dialect. Any female that came close stooped very low. The titled men greeted the Fon by bending low and clapping their hands respectfully three times. The whole scene was worth watching, and I advise all adventurous Americans to take a trip to this palace. Out of the palace I insisted on strolling round and taking in the beautiful scenery.

"The women here are very hardworking," said Tampia. The soil is very infertile and they have to work very hard to reap the little they get."

We got back to Bamenda before dark and I resisted all attempts by Tampia to go drinking that night. I was now thinking of my trip back to America. I had purchased a few interesting pieces of art and some traditional garments. My camera was full of pictures and I was now prepared to show my father back in America what I had learned. My carton of Kola Coffee was the bulkiest item I had collected. I had enough coffee to last me till Kola Coffee would be easily found in any shop in Boston.

The trip back to Douala was comfortable. The honourable gentleman had again obliged us with one of his cars, so we were stopped only once by gendarmes. After a few headaches at the airport, I finally boarded the plane and was on my way to America.

"Welcome home, son," my father boomed as I stepped into the living room. He was reclining on a chair watching one of his favourite TV shows, and I perceived that he did not want to be disturbed. I took out a packet of Kola Coffee and asked the servant to brew some. Then I dropped into a seat next to my father and waited for him to have time for me.

"You abandoned me out there without money," I accused.

After ignoring me and concentrating on the TV for a while he finally turned round smiling.

"You had a good time I suppose."

"If it were just the coffee, yes I had a good time."

"Is that all you can remember about Cameroon, coffee?"

"Well..."

"Well?" questioned my father.

"Well I wouldn't like to live in Cameroon as a poor man."

"Did you see why they think America is a heaven and abandon everything to come here?"

"There is real misery out there," I replied. "From police harassment and corruption to abject poverty."

"But don't you think they should stay back and fix things instead of escaping to America?"

"Go to Cameroon and you will see that there is very little they can do," I said.

"I am glad you have understood their plight," my father finally said smiling. I did not spend money for nothing."

"I have realized that African countries are in real trouble." I continued in a bid to prove to my father that I was not moving with my eyes closed. "And all the bad presidents are protected by the fact that they are surrounded by greedy stooges and a heavily bribed military. What makes everything worse is the position of the superpowers. They are either protecting neo-colonial possessions like the French, looking for a way to penetrate like the Chinese, or simply opposing the other side like the Russians. The Americans who should have stepped in to impose democracy in these countries foolishly believe in the sovereignty of these states. I tell you, Father, until developed and democratic countries such as America, Britain and Germany come together and impose democracy in Africa by force, development will be stifled and a great catastrophe might one day befall the world."

My father was surprised by what I said.

"You seem to have become an expert on Africa," he said. "While foreign relations are important, our think tanks tell us that social and economic development must also be driven from within."

"I visited only one country," I said. "But from very intelligent discussions I gathered from simple persons in small run down bars, I could make out much. Do you know, for example that the leaders in North African countries are relatively worse than those in equatorial Africa?"

"How can that be?" my father asked. "North African countries are far more developed and equatorial Africa has always been plagued by high corruption and poor governance."

"Maybe the North African leaders have better development policies," I replied, "but I learnt out there that their presidents, like the case of Libya and Algeria, are virtually life presidents."

"A life president who brings development is better than a life president that brings nepotism and favours a certain group of stooges, thus ending up with an artificial super rich class, while plunging the rest of the country into misery and underdevelopment," my father said.

"Time changes, Dad and things come round. Time will tell, Dad."

As I sat in my bedroom that night reflecting on my African trip, it occurred to me that my next days were going to be quite busy. All my friends were certainly going to take up my time with questions on my Cameroon trip. I even imagined how some of my lecturers would want me to talk about the trip to the class. The, a thought struck me. I should simply write a book and make it available for everybody to read.

I hope you enjoyed reading it and now know much more about Cameroon than the simple fact that it is a great football country.